At the same time [...] [...] [...] lungs, Jenna's ey[...] [...]pped [...] Blackness surrounded her; panic [...] in instantly as soft whimpers set off a series of echoes. It took a moment for it to sink in the sounds were her own.

Raising both hands, her palms struck a hard object not a foot above her head. She slid her palms over a rough surface, searching, feeling across the top and down the sides of what felt like a wooden crate.

That embodied her like a tomb.

She let go a shriek, crying out in agony, "No! no! please, no!" There was no doubt she was in the very place that stoked the deepest fear in her heart. Just the way her vision forewarned. She was buried alive.

Praise for Donnette Smith

"The author craftily drops bits and pieces, like breadcrumbs for us to follow until the plot is fully revealed."

~ Oya Pearl.

~*~

"Mrs. Smith presents subplots with expert timing, allowing the reader a chance to catch their breath."

~ Jack S

~*~

"I highly recommend this book to anyone looking for an original story that is well written and crisp!"

~ T.G Reaper

~*~

"I could not stop reading this book. It is filled with Mystery, and Love. It keeps you guessing. What will happen next? I can't wait for her next book."

~ Linda Barbane

Dedication

When I think of dedications for Buried Alive, the first person who comes to mind is my fabulous editor at The Wild Rose Press, Kaycee John. She is the one who encouraged me to write my first series. And so, I find myself embarking on this exciting journey to keep Jenna Langley and Cole Rainwater running around in my imagination. I would like to thank all my fans who regularly participate in my contests and are always supportive and encouraging in my writing endeavors. Kellie Griffin, my dear niece, I can't tell you how much I appreciate your support and your generous spirit for sharing my work with others. And thanks to the one person in my life who has been my everything since my teenage years, my husband, Allen. He patiently sits without my company so many nights so that I can create adventures and bring characters to life. He doesn't know that he is the gentleness, the humor, and the courage in all my male heroes.

Chapter One

The woman in the wooden crate pounded her fist against the ceiling. High pitched shrills echoed off the walls. "No! no! no! Oh God, please…somebody get me out of here!"

Her voice caught on a long, desperate whimper. The strong odor of pine wood mixed with human urine overpowered the dank air inside the makeshift casket, making Jenna Langley sick to her stomach, and bringing with it the awful realization the woman had been confined to this space for quite some time.

Claustrophobia threatened to cut off her air like a boa constrictor. Being in this dark grave for only a minute witnessing the suffering of this poor soul sent feral panic racing through Jenna's veins. She couldn't imagine being caged in here this way, buried in the ground, waiting to die.

Although this wasn't Jenna's fate—it was a premonition given to her, an open window to the future by way of a dream—this was a reality for the person left alone in this box to die. It didn't matter how many clairvoyant visions she received. Each one had been as terrifying as the first. And the people who were the target of her premonitions were not a figment of her imagination. Their deadly ordeals were as real as the rising sun.

Loud beeping erupted inside the crate, startling the

victim, causing her breathing to increase. The beeping stopped, and a dim light toward the foot of the pine box snapped on, putting off as much light as the striking of a lighter in a pitch-black cave would have. The faint humming of a fan reverberated against the walls, and infrared digits blinked from the ceiling, just above the woman's face. Jenna recognized the contraption as a time clock, counting down two hours.

The victim let out a tortured wail. "God, please don't let me die. I just want to see him one more time."

As the thought of who the woman could be referring to swirled around Jenna's mind, she gazed down at the victim's tormented face. The light radiating from the bulb at the foot of the casket allowed Jenna just enough of a visual to recognize the eyes she stared into were her own. She gasped, and the realization of who the woman wanted to see one last time exploded through her like a rocket.

"Cole!" Jenna screamed, bolting up in bed.

Cole stirred in the bed next to her. "What…what is it?"

Her breathing came fast as she clicked on the bedside lamp and struggled to speak. "I…I saw myself in a…a casket buried in the ground."

"What?" His arm wrapped around her shoulders. "What happened?"

"Somebody put me in a wooden box. They buried me and put a timeclock in there with me. It was counting down from two hours. I heard a fan blowing from somewhere inside. I…I think when the timeclock reached zero, the fan in the box would cut off. I wanted so badly to see you one more time before I died."

Tears streamed down her face, and Cole drew her

into his arms. "It's okay, honey. It was just a dream. You're not going to die. And I'm right here. I'm not going anywhere. I promise."

She shook her head, shrinking away from him. "After what happened last time, how can you say it was just a dream?"

He stared at her, as if willing her to listen to reason. "Jenna, my father has been dead for more than five months now. He can't hurt you ever again."

"I know that," she said, slipping out of bed and heading toward the bathroom.

Jenna reentered the room, donning a robe and tying the sash. "You know better than anyone what happens when I get these premonitions."

"That's not going to happen this time."

"How do you know?"

"Who would do that to you and why?"

She peered down, shaking her head. "I don't know. But every time I've had one of these visions, it has come true."

"You're right," he admitted, getting up, grabbing his boxer shorts off the floor, and sliding into them. He approached Jenna, taking her by the arm, and gently twirling her to face him. "I would give anything to take back what my father did to you, what he did to our daughter. I wish I would have known he was still alive, that he planned to go after you and Emily. I feel so badly for not believing you when you were having all those visions. I could have prevented everything if I'd have just listened to you."

She shook her head adamantly. "None of that was your fault. You couldn't have known your father was running around killing women. We all thought he committed suicide by setting himself on fire in that van years ago. Even the authorities were convinced of it. There was no way for us to know he was still alive and planned to kill me and kidnap Emily."

Cole rested his chin on top of her head. "I thank God every day you and Emily are safe."

"It's because of you that we are. You rescued us. Me and Emily are so lucky to have you."

He squeezed her tight, then released her, kissing her forehead. "Know what I think? Our wedding is only a few weeks away. And you have been working tirelessly making sure every detail is taken care of, all while recuperating from your car accident. Perhaps the stress of all of this was the cause of your bad dream."

"It wasn't a dream."

She stepped over to the window, stood in front of it, and gazed out into the darkness. What if it was happening all over again? The haunting visions, and then the dead bodies being discovered soon after. Was she a fool to have believed the death of Joseph Rainwater would bring an end to this nightmare? The man was gone with a bullet in his head. The medical examiner pronounced him dead at the scene. Cole was right, he couldn't hurt her.

But somebody wanted to.

"It was too real to be a dream," she admitted more to herself than to Cole.

"What about that professor you told me about. The one you consulted with when you were having your visions before?"

She peered at him. "You mean Professor Delaney?"

"The one from the Paranormal Research Center."

"What about her?"

"If this is worrying you, maybe you should go see her."

Jenna munched on her lip. The woman had certainly been a tremendous help the last time. There was a possibility the professor could apply her knowledge on the subject and decipher the meaning of this disturbing vision. "You know, I think that's the best idea you've ever had."

"I get those sometimes. It may be purely accidental though."

She grinned, spinning on her heels to face him. "Even dipshits have their moments."

"Hey," he said, coming toward Jenna mischievously. He took her by the waist, lifting her into the air. "I'll have you know I resemble that."

Jenna chuckled, staring into his eyes as he slid her back down. "You mean, you resent that."

"No, I meant resemble."

She pursed her lips. "So, you agree you're a dipshit?"

"Now that was just uncalled for."

"What? You were the one who said it."

"I said it to make you laugh. You weren't supposed to agree."

"Oh, yeah? So, what are you going to do about it?"

He gazed into her eyes until the reflection of jest in his transformed into desire. "First I'm going to kiss you," he said, capturing her lips in a slow, lazy caress.

The tingling sensation spiraled from Jenna's head down to her toes. It had always been this way every time Cole touched her. He had the commanding ability to turn her insides into jelly. And he didn't even have to put an ounce of effort into it.

He dragged his lips down the inside of her neck, saying in a husky voice, "Then I'm going to drag you over to that bed and seduce you. Any objections?"

"I would object if you didn't."

"I knew you'd see things my way," he said, sweeping her into his arms and carrying her over to the bed.

Even as the love of her life carted her toward the bed for some midnight indulgence, the memory of her earlier dream burned in her gut. The sooner the professor could be contacted, the quicker she could get some answers. Hopefully, Cole was right, and this incident was nothing more than a nightmare brought on by stress.

****

It was nine a.m. by the time Cole strolled through the doors of the Farmersville PD. He would have been here an hour earlier if he hadn't overslept. It was Jenna's fault. Between the nightmare and the lovemaking, a few hours' sleep was all a guy could manage. But exhausted or not, it had been worth every minute. He found sleep a rare commodity ever since the day she'd moved her belongings into his house. At some point they would have to barricade themselves from each other to get on with a normal, productive life. He hoped that day would never come.

"Glad you finally decided to join us, detective," Jeremy Gibbs, his partner at the precinct said, as Cole ambled toward his office. "There's an attorney who has been calling you for the past hour."

"What attorney?"

Gibbs shrugged. "How am I supposed to know?

His number is on your desk."

Cole stepped into his office and glanced at the note sitting on his desk. *The Carter Law Firm. Contact Jim Carter.* He took note of the phone number, sat down, and snatched up the phone.

After two rings a woman answered. "The Carter Law Firm. How can I direct your call?"

"This is Detective Cole Rainwater. I have a message that Jim Carter wanted to speak with me. Is he in?"

"Let me transfer you."

"Good morning, Detective Rainwater. This is Jim Carter speaking. I'm glad you called me back."

"Sure," Cole said, wondering what on Earth the man wanted.

"I'm the successor trustee for your great-grandfather's will. He passed away last month, and I—"

"Let me stop you right there. My father, who is now deceased, was put into foster care from infancy. He was never adopted out, and the identity of his parents are unknown to this day. You have the wrong person, Mr. Carter."

"I assure you I don't, Mr. Rainwater. You are the son of Joseph Rainwater, correct? According to my sources, you were raised by your uncle, Derek Rainwater, after your father was placed in a psychiatric ward. Is that correct?"

Now the man had Cole's attention. "Those are some pretty good sources you have."

"I wouldn't have made this call if I didn't know for certain you are the person I need to speak with."

"Okay. So, who is this great-grandfather I never knew existed?"

"His name was Hershel Rainwater. He owned two estates and was a sixty percent shareholder in a very lucrative business. You've heard of Toys Galore?"

"I believe they're one of the biggest toy distributors in the United States."

"And abroad. Your great-grandfather started the company twenty years ago."

"So, why are you calling me? I've never even met the man."

"Hershel had two beneficiaries named in his trust. You are one of them."

Cole's brows furrowed. "I don't understand. I've never laid eyes on the man. Why would he list me as a beneficiary in his trust?"

"I'd like to say it was done out of obligation and a sense of selflessness. But Hershel Rainwater was a narcissist. He was well known for his ruthless behavior. He was one of those guys you didn't cross unless you were willing to have your life turned upside-down."

So much for beating around the bush. "Sounds like a real sweetheart. So, what was it about me, a great-grandson he never interacted with, that caused him to have a change of heart?"

"It wasn't you. It was a guilty conscience eating at him after all these years. His daughter was raped. Years after her death he capitalized on that rape. He never forgave himself for it."

Being that Cole's father had turned out to be a serial killer, he imagined cold heartedness must run in his family. "I'm going to have to ask for an explanation."

"I figured. Hershel's daughter, Jasmine worked as an intern for a well-known senator. She was raped and impregnated by that same man and later died. Hershel waited until after her death to blackmail the senator. He offered the politician an ultimatum. Either he could pay Hershel a substantial amount of money, or he planned to go to the media with the truth. He had proof of the rape."

An image of Cole's young daughter, Emily flashed before his eyes. He couldn't imagine doing anything so unforgiveable to her. He'd kill any bastard who was brave enough to harm one hair on her head. He let out a whoosh. "I see. I'm betting Jasmine was my grandmother."

"Yes."

"And what about the child she was pregnant with?"

"You mean children."

"Twins?"

"Two boys. She put them up for adoption. She refused to report the rape. The senator was a powerful man with a lot of influence, and she was afraid of what he would do to her if she went to authorities."

"Ahh. My father, Joseph, and my uncle, Derek, were the twin boys she put up for adoption."

"That's right."

"You said there were two beneficiaries named in Hershel's trust. Who is the other one?"

"Your younger brother, Dunston Rainwater."

Cole drew the phone away from his ear and stared at the receiver. How in the hell did he have a brother all these years and didn't know about it? "So, now you're telling me I have a younger brother? You're just full of surprises, Mr. Carter."

"Your mother, Charlotte was pregnant when she abandoned the home she and Joseph shared years ago.

She left a few weeks after the authorities had Joseph committed to a psychiatric hospital. Of course, she didn't know she was pregnant at the time."

If his mother had dealt with Dunston the same way she dealt with Cole—abandoning him to the possibility of becoming a ward of the state—there was no telling what kind of upbringing the kid suffered through. Fortunately, his psychotic father had enough sense to bring him to his twin brother's doorstep, Derek, to raise when he was a toddler. Cole chalked it up to the only meaningful thing his father had ever done for him. Then the man went on a killing spree that spanned more than eighteen years. Cole still cringed every time the memory of the atrocious deeds his father had committed surfaced. He imagined the shock and dismay of those discoveries would never go away.

"Listen, I'm going to be in my office around three o'clock today. Would it be possible for you to meet me here? We need to sort through Mr. Rainwater's trust."

Cole frowned, leaning back in his chair. "To be honest, Mr. Carter—"

"Call me Jim."

"Okay, Jim. I don't have any interest in anything Hershel might have left for me after his death. I didn't know he existed, and apparently, I wasn't important enough for him to have sought me out when he was still alive. I'd prefer not to be a part of whatever guilt he harbored that made him feel he needed to leave an estranged great-grandson an inheritance. I've done just fine so far without him or his money, or whatever it is he felt obligated to leave me. I do have a question though."

"Shoot."

"How the hell did you know where to find me?"

"Mr. Rainwater paid a lot of money to certain folks to keep tabs on you and your brother over the years."

Cole grinned derisively, fighting the urge to hang up the phone. With all Hershel's resources, he never thought to reach out to him or Cole's newfound brother. "It seems to me he had more money than he had sense. After all, it appears he missed the most important thing in life. Family. His money couldn't buy the people who mattered most."

"I can't argue with that. Jasmine's mother died giving birth to her, and Hershel never remarried. He had no close friends. He was a lonely man surrounded by his things."

"We all make our choices, don't we?"

"Indeed. I'm not sure what to do with your inheritance, Mr. Rainwater. I didn't anticipate this reaction. I've already talked to your brother, and he plans to be here at three o'clock."

Cole didn't expect that. "My brother is in town, then?"

"He's rented a room at the inn in McKinney."

Even if he wasn't interested in the inheritance a bitter, old man left him, he was intrigued by the prospect of meeting a brother he just learned he had. Both his father and uncle were dead. And now he learned his grandmother, as well as his great-grandfather were also deceased. His family tree was rapidly shedding its leaves.

"Tell you what, Jim. Give me the address and I'll be there."

"Great," the attorney said, rattling off the location of his office.

When Cole got off the phone, he didn't know how to feel about this latest discovery. In a few hours, he would be face to face with his younger brother. Perhaps, some good had come out of this after all.

His eyes brushed across the *best Dad in the world* mug sitting on his desk. His nine-year-old daughter had bought it for him while on a shopping excursion with her mother. He couldn't control the pride that rose in his chest at the memory of how she'd hid it behind her back and presented it to him with an enormous smile that instantly lit up his world. He had bent down and kissed the tip of her nose, told her he would treasure it forever, and thanked her for thinking of him. It was beyond him how any man could do to his daughter what Hershel had done to Jasmine. Emily and Jenna were his whole world. There was no length he wouldn't go to protect them.

A phone jingled out in the bullpen, snapping him back to reality. His partner's gruff voice told him who had snatched up the receiver and answered the call. There was no time to sit around wondering what made Hershel such a callous man. He had his life to live, a wedding to plan, and a brother to meet.

****

The moment Jenna entered the door of her office, her cell phone rang. She dug it out of her purse and glanced at the screen. Barbara Cassidy's name appeared. She smiled, sliding her finger across the phone to answer the call. "Hey, there, bestie," she chirped, ambling to her desk and dropping her purse onto it.

"I thought you'd be interested to know I'm in the middle of planning your wedding shower. And I've found the perfect place to host it."

"I love that you're taking your maid of honor duties seriously, but Cole refuses to let my father pay for the wedding, remember? And with us about to put a down payment on the ranch, I figured we'd skip the expense of a shower."

"Not on your life, sister. I'm paying for it."

"I will not let you do that."

"Since when have you ever been able to stop me from doing anything?"

Good point. "I really wish you wouldn't though. It will only make Cole feel terrible."

"It's not every day my best friend gets married. Cole is a big boy. He'll get over it. You can consider this my wedding gift to you."

It would be a waste of energy to fight Barbara on this, or anything else for that matter. The woman was every bit as stubborn as Cole. She imagined that had been the reason the two clashed so often. "All right. So where is this perfect place?"

"As if I'd tell you and ruin the surprise."

"So why did you call me with this news in the first place?"

"I didn't want you to forget how awesome a friend I am."

Sounded about right. Jenna chuckled, sitting down at her desk and powering up the computer. "Listen, do you remember that professor you invited to my house when I was having all those out of body experiences?"

"Professor Delaney from the Paranormal Research Center?"

"Yeah. She gave me her business card, but I can't seem to find it. Do you have her number?"

"Why?"

"I need to get in touch with her."

"Because?"

"I'm inviting her to the wedding."

"Bullshit. Are you having visions again?"

"Ugh." Why couldn't she ever get away with hiding anything from Barbara? Although she loved and trusted her best friend, the woman had a way of involving herself in the affairs of others, especially when her participation was unwanted. Besides, Jenna didn't want to alarm anyone. She preferred to keep her latest clairvoyant episode under wraps until she had an opportunity to discuss it with the professor.

"I have her number. I'll give it to you after you tell me what's going on."

"You're really going to hold her number hostage?"

"You bet I am."

"Why do I put up with you?"

"Because you love me. Besides, you know I can help. So, spill it."

"All right, fine. I had a crazy dream last night that I was buried alive in a makeshift casket. Cole seems to think the dream was caused by stress of the upcoming wedding."

Barbara didn't say anything for a minute, and then, "This is going to sound crazy, but for once I agree with him. That kind of stress can bring on unusual dreams."

"I don't have dreams like normal people. Mine are premonitions of things to come. You of all people know that."

"Jenna, the threat is gone. I don't see any reason why you should be having visions of being buried alive. I know you're clairvoyant, but you are also human. And people have nightmares that are, well…just nightmares. Undue stress causes bad dreams."

"And how would you know?"

"Because when you were having all those episodes the last time, I did a little research into the symbolic meaning of dreams."

"So, you're going to give me your expert opinion on what this dream means."

"I'll leave that to the professor. I'll text you her number."

"Thank you."

"I think it's great you're going to talk to her. But I wouldn't read too much into the occurrence. You've got a lot on your plate right now. The best thing you can do is stay calm and focused."

"Thanks for the advice, Dr. Cassidy."

"Anytime. I think we should go have a drink. Relax. Unwind. We've hardly spent any time together since your accident."

"I know. It took a lot longer than I anticipated to recover."

"You broke your thigh bone. Did you think you'd be dancing within a month?"

"I didn't expect it to take five months."

"What did the doctor tell you?"

"Yeah, yeah. I know. But I've fully recuperated now, thank God."

"Good, because if you don't have a drink with me, I'm going to kidnap you."

"I will. I promise. Text me her number."

"Doing it right now."

"Bye."

"Talk to ya later."

As soon as the text popped up, Jenna dialed the number to the professor's cell phone. She had to admit, Barbara's reaction to her disturbing dream put her mind at ease. Her friend had the same response Cole did. Perhaps they were right, and stress was the culprit. She could only hope. Either way, after meeting with Professor Delaney, she'd find out soon enough.

****

Leaning against the doorframe and quietly studying the movements of her handsome fiancé sent a flutter rising in her chest. Unaware of her presence, Cole shuffled through a file on his desk. His suit jacket was draped over his chair, and the cuffs of his white shirt, rolled up to his elbows. And Jenna couldn't stop staring at the smooth muscles in his forearms. When he finally peered up, warmth simmered in his eyes.

"Hey, you," he said, closing the file and shoving it to the side. "How long have you been standing there?"

"Long enough to decide I have the best-looking fiancé in all of Texas."

"Ha," he said, getting up and sauntering over to her. "That's bullshit and we both know it."

"Really," she responded, allowing him to back her up against the wall. Her heart picked up the pace the moment he leaned into her face and whispered huskily, "The reason you want to marry me, honey, has nothing to do with my looks."

"Then what could it be?" she asked, breathlessly.

He slid his warm hand up her bare arm, leaving goosebumps it its wake. "It's because I give one helluva mean massage."

"We can save a lot of money in massage therapy."

"I can cook, too."

"What else can you do?"

"I'm good at solving mysteries," he confessed, brushing a stray curl away from her cheek, and then framing her face with his hand and running his thumb along her jawline and up to her bottom lip.

"What am I thinking right now, mystery solver?"

He bent close to her ear and said, "You're wondering how it would feel if you were naked and I was on top of you."

An icy hot sensation ripped through her. And she broke out in an instant sweat.

"You're looking a little peaked. Maybe I should take you home?"

Someone swept past his office door and yelled, "Get a room!"

Cole grinned devilishly as he stared deep into her eyes, penetrating her soul. "I couldn't agree more."

Jenna cleared her throat. "I was thinking about lunch. I'm starved."

"Did I mention I can cook?"

"Not today, stud."

He groaned, backing away from her. "So, where are we off to?"

"Our favorite little Mexican cantina."

His brows raised. "The last time we were there, you got angry at me and ran off without eating."

"That's true. It was the second time we'd seen each other after being away for ten years. But it was then I realized my feelings for you were stronger than they were when we were teenagers."

"You had a funny way of showing that."

"You pissed me off."

"Maybe I should piss you off more often."

"I wouldn't recommend it."

"Are we taking my truck, then?"

She nodded and they headed toward the exit together.

Chapter Two

Once they arrived at the cantina, they chose a small table situated in the corner, away from other patrons. The server carried over menus and took their drink orders.

"What, no margarita this time?" Cole remarked, grinning.

His words awakened a particular scene from the last time they were here. It had been a little over five months ago, and Jenna couldn't believe time went by so quickly. Back then Cole had taken the liberty of ordering her a margarita before she'd arrived at the restaurant. She was so nervous only having seen him for the second time in ten years, she feared one alcoholic drink would not be enough to get her through it. "You didn't exactly invite me out for a date that night, remember?"

"Even though my intention was to find out how you knew about the first murder victim before we'd found the body, I was still excited to see you, and just as nervous as the first time I took you on a date when we were fifteen."

"That so?" A thrill shot through her. "You didn't seem like a bundle of nerves the night you asked me here."

"I'm a detective. Playing it cool and hiding my emotions comes with the territory."

"I have to be honest; I was surprised coming back to Texas after so long to discover you were a homicide detective."

"Not as surprised as I was to realize you were having clairvoyant visions of the murders I was investigating."

She grinned, opening the menu and scanning it, too preoccupied to pay much attention to the entrees. "You didn't believe me at first."

"I think deep down I did. But the fact you saw the murders in advance defied logic. In the homicide division, we go on evidence we can see. Your visions didn't fit that mold."

She lowered her head. "I often wonder how different things may have been if my parents hadn't swept me away to Georgia when they found out I was pregnant. You wouldn't have missed out on knowing our daughter for so long. I regret not telling you about Emily more than you can ever know."

Her hand tingled where the warmth of his covered hers. He gently squeezed and said, "You were seventeen years old when that happened. I was going through so much at the time, finding out the man I thought was my father was a serial killer, and then that he committed suicide as the police were closing in on him. I, too, imagined how different things would have been if I'd paid more attention to what was going on with you when your parents ripped us apart. If I had realized you were pregnant with Emily, I can assure you your parents would have never taken you away from Texas. If I hadn't been so blind, I would have known you still loved me."

"I should have never doubted that."

"Look at me."

When she did, a reflection of warmth and understanding radiated from the depths of his gray eyes. "We were both victims in this. You were a scared, pregnant teenager whose parents did everything they could at the time to keep us apart because they thought my father was a serial killer. And I was a confused young man who had lost his girlfriend at the same time he had to come to terms with his father's suicide and the horrific crimes he had committed."

"It had to be a relief for you when the truth came out and you realized the man who raised you, your uncle Derek, wasn't the person who killed those women."

"To be honest, even when the police found my uncle dead in his van with the bodies of those two kidnapped girls, I had my doubts about his capabilities to do such a thing. He wasn't that kind of person. Derek was a gentle man, and a good father to me. It never quite added up, ya know? So, the day my father, Joseph, kidnapped our daughter to get to you, and I tracked him down to his house, although I was shocked when he admitted he murdered my uncle and set it up to look like he had killed those women, it made sense given Derek's kind nature he was never the serial killer. I just wish my uncle would have told me who my real father was. I spent way too many years believing he was my father."

"I'm just so grateful you got to his house before I did. When Joseph called me and said he was holding Emily hostage, all I could think about was getting there as quickly as I could to save her. If I hadn't gotten into that car accident, I would have shown up over there, and he would have killed me and Emily."

"I know you think I saved her, but the truth is, when he knocked me out and tied me to that chair across the table from Emily, he could have easily killed us both."

"But he didn't. It was because you were his biological son that he couldn't. He didn't expect you to come there. He lured me there by kidnapping Emily. If I would have shown up, we both know what would have happened. So, yes, Cole Rainwater, whether you realize it or not, you saved us."

He frowned, grabbing his menu, and finally opening it as well. "I guess when you put it that way…"

After a few minutes, their server stopped back by and took their orders. Cole asked, "Did you ever get hold of Professor Delaney?"

"We have a meeting scheduled later today."

"Good." He peered at her, his expression transforming into one of seriousness. "I have some interesting news."

"What is it?"

"I got to the station earlier this morning to learn an attorney had been trying to get in touch with me. When I called him back, he told me he was handling the living trust of my great-grandfather, Hershel Rainwater. It seems I have been left an inheritance."

Jenna sat intrigued as Cole laid out the details of who this mystery great-grandfather was and relayed most of the information given to him by this attorney.

"Oh my God, Cole," she said, when she was finally able to speak.

"And that's not even the most interesting part."

"There's more?"

The server approached with their food, and Jenna observed the young man setting the dishes in front of them and asking if they wanted anything else. She briskly shook her head, hoping to send him away quickly so Cole could continue with his news.

He was silent as he took a sip of tea and picked up his fork.

She said, "As you were saying."

"Oh, yeah." He frowned, took a bite, and then said, "What were we talking about?"

She shot him an expression that told him she knew full well he remembered exactly what he was about to mention.

All innocence, he said, "What?"

"Out with it."

He pointed his fork toward her plate. "You should eat. This is really good."

She glared at him the way a school yard bully would stare at a kid with milk money.

"All right, I'll tell you, but only because you're scaring me."

She folded her arms, quite satisfied with herself.

"I have a younger brother. His name is Dunston."

Her mouth opened wide enough to send a train chugging through it.

"Speechless for once?"

"I…you…just came right out with that. I didn't expect you to say that."

"I feared for my life."

"Be serious, Cole."

"I am. You looked like you were going to hurt me."

"So, who is this guy?"

"I don't know. But he will be at the meeting today with the attorney. It's honestly the only reason I'm going."

She sat back in her chair, doing her best to digest this unexpected information. "Wow," she said, blown away. "This is exciting news, isn't it?"

"I really don't know yet. I haven't met him. Would you like to go with me?"

"Hell, yes." She gave him a wink. "I wonder if he's as handsome as you."

He shook his head. "The older brother is always more handsome."

She let out a lighthearted snort. "How do you know that?"

"Don't you watch movies? According to Hollywood, the older brother gets the leading roles. They always get the girl. They are the smartest, strongest, and best looking. You know it's true."

Her attention floated toward the ceiling. "I bet he's not as big-headed as you, though."

"That's only because he's not marrying the most fascinating…" He took her hand and put it to his lips, kissing one finger, "most intelligent…" He kissed a second and third finger, "most sexy woman in all of Texas."

A fiery sensation shot through her, and she snatched her hand away. She imagined her face was flushed. "You really can't do that in public."

He grinned devilishly, winking at her. "Why, does it make you want to jump my bones?"

She glanced away, doing her best to keep her composure, then cleared her throat. "What time is your meeting?"

"Three o'clock."

"Darn."

"Why? What's the problem?"

"That's the same time I have to meet with Professor Delaney."

"Oh."

"I'll just cancel the meeting."

He shook his head. "I don't think that's a good idea. I could tell the dream you had last night really upset you. I think you should go."

"But I—"

"Listen. It's no big deal. I'll meet with the attorney and my long lost brother, and you go see the professor. You'll feel better if you do."

She considered it for a minute, deciding Cole was probably right. The sooner she got to the bottom of her disturbing dream, the better she'd feel. She remembered how relieved she'd been when the professor agreed to meet with her on such short notice. As excited as she was for Cole and the news he had a brother he'd never met, she was as equally concerned about the possible dark prediction of her dream.

"Okay," she said, making up her mind. "I'll go see Professor Delaney. But if you need me, I'll just be a phone call away."

"Cole Rainwater, is that you?"

Jenna looked up to find a slender, blonde woman standing over her fiancé. "My word, I thought that was you. How in the world have you been?"

"Ava," Cole said, recognition reflecting in his eyes. "I've been okay. How about you?"

The tall woman shook her head, a showy smile plastered on her face. "I have been just fabulous, darlin'."

Darlin'?

Who was this woman? Jenna didn't appreciate how close she stood to her fiancé, or her cozy reference to him. She cleared her throat, signaling the fact she was sitting there.

"This is my fiancée, Jenna Langley," Cole said, his attention going to her. "Ava is an old friend."

"Is that what you call a former girlfriend?" this Ava said, a bit too surly for Jenna's comfort.

"You two used to date," Jenna said in a statement as opposed to a question.

Cole no sooner opened his mouth to answer before Ava spoke for him. "We were romantically involved for quite some time." She turned, that exaggerated smile once again converging on her features as if she were auditioning for a toothpaste commercial. "In all the years I've known you, Cole, I never would have imagined you'd settle down."

"Excuse me," Jenna said, directing her attention toward the rude woman. "My fiancé has a mouth, and a voice that works fine. He doesn't need your help to answer my question, *darlin'*."

"Pardon me, honey, I—"

"It's Jenna," she said as cool as a cucumber. "Honey is what you drizzle on sopapillas." She gestured toward her plate, where two orders of fried pastry sat on a decorated plate and surrounded by a small clear jug. "See?" she said, pointing at the jug, "this is honey."

When Jenna's gaze drifted over to Cole, he sat back in his chair, an amused grin spread across his face. She said to Ava, "Now if you'll excuse us, our meal is getting cold, but we hope you have a splendid day."

Face turned to stone, Ava spun on one heel and stormed off without another word.

In a move that surprised Jenna, Cole leaned back in his chair and laughed.

She said, "What's so funny?"

"Remind me never to spar with you."

"She was getting on my nerves."

"I could see that."

Jenna sliced into her enchilada with a little more force than she'd intended. "What manner of intelligence could that woman have brought to any relationship you ever had with her?"

"I wasn't dating her for her brains, darlin'."

"Oh, I see. She's pretty. So, that's what it was all about, huh?"

He smirked. "Pretty much."

"Good grief. Why do men use women like that?"

"Trust me, she used me far more than I did her."

Jenna sighed, the anger previously welling inside ebbing a bit. She believed him. "She definitely looks like the type who would."

"Jealous?"

She snorted. "Of that? A snail has more brains than she does."

"So, you *are* jealous."

She took a bite, chewed, swallowed, and shrugged. "Okay, maybe a little."

"There's no reason to be. The truth is when you left, I couldn't have a serious relationship with anyone. No one measured up to you. You were the love of my life from the day I met you. But you were gone for ten years. A man gets lonely from time to time. That's all

Ava ever was."

She peered down at the table and had to admit, she'd had a few of those herself over the years. It was unrealistic to expect he'd been celibate all that time. She certainly hadn't been.

He stretched one big hand across the table, covering hers with one palm and twining their fingers into a firm knot. "I love you, Jenna Langley, with all my heart. I've got you and Emily. I am right where I'm meant to be. I don't need anyone to fill the void anymore."

Her heart swelled with love for this man. He had been everything she'd ever needed, and ever since they'd found each other again, her life was set on the right course. "I feel the same way."

"Good. Let's eat. Our meal is getting cold."

****

Cole checked his watch as he trudged up the stairs of the Isaac Building and sauntered through the double glass doors. He was five minutes early. He found the Carter Law Firm on the third floor and rode the elevator up. As the doors slid open, butterflies danced in his stomach. All this time he assumed he'd been an only child. What would he say to his new-found brother? His mind formed a dozen images of Dunston. Would they favor one another? Or would his brother resemble the mother he never met? As he treaded down the hall, pausing at each door to check the suite numbers, those thoughts heightened, and nervousness made his palms sweaty. When he finally stood in front of suite 397, he put his hand on the doorknob, took a deep breath, and swung open the door.

Cole peered around the room. A small sofa, along

with two high-backed chairs served as the only furniture. He noticed a few colorful, painted canvases hanging from the walls. Then he zeroed in on a dark-haired woman sitting behind a glass partition. She smiled, saying, "Are you Mr. Rainwater?"

He approached. "I'm supposed to meet Mr. Carter. I know I'm a few minutes early."

"They're in there." She pointed toward the only other door. "You can go on back."

He nodded his appreciation and stepped through the entryway.

There were two men in the room. They both glanced up when he entered. The older fellow with the glasses, sitting behind the desk, must have been Mr. Carter. And the one seated across the room to the right was unmistakably his brother. The young man had the same cleft chin as Joseph and Derek Rainwater, the one feature Cole did not inherit. But he had the same gray eyes and receding hairline as the Rainwater twins and Cole. Only, Dunston had a thick head of blond hair, unlike the black hair Cole shared with his uncle and father. He had no doubt his brother must have gotten his hair color from their mother, Charlotte.

Jim cleared his throat. "I'm glad you could join us. Me and Dunston were hopeful you'd make it. Why don't you have a seat," he said, gesturing toward the chair on the opposite side of the room.

At a loss for words, Cole sat.

But Dunston piped up, "You look nothing like I imagined."

Cole turned in the chair to face his brother. "Did the blond hair come from our mother?"

"Have you ever met her?"

"No."

"Lucky you."

"About as charming as dear, ol' dad, huh?"

"She hasn't made a hobby out of killing people. At least not that I'm aware of. But she kicked me out of the house when I was fifteen to move in some guy she just met. Turned out he didn't like kids. Especially the teenage kind. So, whatever she's done after that point, I wouldn't know."

"Our parents' strong suit was not child-rearing."

Dunston nodded and frowned as if he couldn't argue with that. "I'm guessing the black hair came from Dad."

"The same person you got those eyes and that chin from."

The attorney cleared his throat. "I know this is the first time you two have seen each other, but I have a client scheduled for a meeting within the hour. At the expense of not sounding rude, we really need to get on with this."

Both men quieted as Jim Carter opened a file on his desk. After a moment of scanning the documents, he leveled his attention on the two of them. "Your great-grandfather, Hershel Rainwater, owned two estates in Texas. The Blazing Saddle Ranch, named after his prized stallion, Blaze. This is a three-hundred-acre ranch located in Dallas. The property has a twelve-thousand square foot mansion. Hershel left this estate to Cole, along with an inheritance of five million dollars."

Cole was positive his jaw must have hit the floor.

"The other estate," Carter went on, "is in Arlington. It's an eight-thousand square foot manor on one-hundred-twenty acres of land. Dunston will inherit this property along with one million dollars."

Cole wondered why Hershel didn't evenly split the money between him and his brother. But before he could ponder it further, the attorney said, "Hershel owned a few, smaller plots of land in two states. Those are to be sold and the proceeds split among three different charities Hershel supported, along with the remainder of his money."

Carter then grabbed two manila envelopes sitting off to the side, rose from his desk, and carried one over to Cole and the other to Dunston. "Your great-grandfather also left these for you both. The keys to the estates you have inherited are also in those envelopes." The attorney returned to his seat, and announced, "If either one of you are unsatisfied with your inheritance, you are certainly entitled to fight it in court. If this is the path you choose to take, I will warn you a living trust such as this one is very difficult to contest. They are designed that way. The chances you will be victorious are slim to none. And the cost for doing so is quite high."

Cole first glanced at his brother, who sat expressionless, staring straight ahead at the attorney. He then ripped open the envelope, drawing out a set of keys and a one-page letter signed by his great grandfather.

Cole,

If my sources are right about you, you're probably thinking I can go straight to Hell, even though I just made you a rich man.

I don't blame you. I could have reached out to you, but I never did. I could go into a dozen reasons why, but I won't waste your time. Let's just say I'm not a good person. I've done a lot of things I regret. And if you had become a part of my life, I would have only made you regret ever knowing me.

I am turning over my company shares to you. You are now 60% owner of Toys Galore. Sebastian Sawyer will be in touch. He is one of the three shareholders and has been instructed to counsel you on my behalf and on behalf of the company. Don't let him bullshit you. He will try.

There are a few reasons I have entrusted my shares with you instead of your brother. You are more mature and more responsible than Dunston. You have created a stable life for yourself despite the unfortunate hand you have been given. I have faith in your ability to make good, sound decisions. You are a father, and soon to become a husband. And you deserve this opportunity.

I wish you the best.

Hershel Rainwater

Cole folded the letter and stuffed it back into the envelope, reeling from this bizarre circumstance. He didn't have a clue how to go about digesting all of this. His life transformed drastically within the last thirty minutes. He became a rich man, and the owner of a lucrative company. And all of it happened so quickly. His attention drifted toward Dunston, who held his envelope upside down, sending a set of keys, as well as another shiny object sliding into his palm. Cole couldn't believe his eyes as he stared at his uncle's dog tags.

Dunston dipped his hand into the envelope, checking for additional items. It was empty. He turned to the attorney, held up the dog tags, and shrugged, saying, "What the hell is this?"

Cole answered for him. "Those belonged to Derek Rainwater. Our father stole them from him. In fact, some of Joseph's victims described those dog tags hanging around his neck when he committed his crimes."

"Why in the world would I want them?"

Cole frowned, shaking his head. The more important questions would have been, why did Hershel give Dunston the dog tags their biological father wore while committing murder? Cole recalled his father Joseph was wearing them the day he kidnapped Emily to lure Jenna to his house. Not able to kill his son, Joseph turned the gun on himself as police sirens wailed in the distance. So, if the dog tags were around his father's neck at the time of his suicide, how did their great-grandfather end up with them?

Dropping the dog tags back into the envelope, Dunston asked Cole, "What did you get?"

"A letter." At this time, he figured the less information he offered, the better. At least until he had time to make sense of this unexpected manifestation.

"Gentlemen, I think this wraps up our business for today," Jim said, nodding curtly at them. "I'll be in touch next week and we will set up a wire transfer for the inheritance."

As Cole stood and issued a goodbye to Mr. Carter and his brother, a million thoughts ran through his mind. Most pressing of them all was the need to share this news with Jenna. Over the last five and a half months they'd grown much closer than they had ever been as teenagers. They'd looked to each other for advice, help in solving problems, and a soulmate with whom to share significant occurrences in their lives.

This latest event certainly fit the bill. She could help him make sense of it all.

Before climbing into his truck and grabbing his phone to call her, he checked his watch. It was only three-forty. He doubted her meeting with the professor had ended. Best not to disturb her just yet.

He slid behind the wheel and fired up the engine, deciding there'd be plenty of time to discuss this matter with her once he had returned home at the end of the day. He couldn't wait to see her.

****

Professor Delaney peered up from the desk as Jenna strolled into her office. "How have you been?" she asked as Jenna took a seat.

Settling into the chair and setting her purse in the opposite seat, Jenna frowned. "Other than this latest dream, I've been great."

"I hear you're about to get married. Congratulations."

"How did you know that?"

"Barbara calls often. She told me."

Of course, she did. The only way to keep her best friend from running her mouth would be to stuff a sock in it, then duct tape it to her face.

"In fact, she called me earlier today right after she talked to you."

"Figures."

"She's only concerned for you."

"That might be, but she's also a blabbermouth."

"I've noticed. She told me all about what happened with Cole's father, Joseph."

"So, you're all up to speed," Jenna said, picturing her hands around Barbara's neck.

"Hard to believe all these years he thought the uncle that raised him was his father, only to find out his biological father was still alive and was the serial killer he'd been investigating."

"If it hadn't been for the first girl Joseph tried to kidnap, and her friend reporting his partial license plate to police, I often wonder if we ever would have found out he was behind all of it."

"It must have been terrifying for you when Joseph called to tell you he kidnapped your daughter."

"He saw me on the news and remembered me as Cole's girlfriend when we were teenagers. He also recalled I was clairvoyant and figured I was seeing the murders he was committing."

"Which you were."

"I wish I could forget, believe me."

"I'm so glad Cole got there before you. He would have killed you."

"He planned on it. That was the whole reason he kidnapped Emily."

The professor folded her hands across the desk, and said, "So, tell me about this latest episode. When we talked briefly over the phone, I understood it to be a dream or vision, not an out-of-body experience like the ones you had before."

"I'm not sure if it was a dream or a vision. It was terrifyingly real. It felt the same as a vision, only I saw it in a dream."

"Tell me what you saw."

"I was inside of a makeshift casket. It was dark, and someone was in there with me. At first, I didn't know who it was. The woman trapped inside was crying and wailing. It seemed as if she had been in there awhile. I could hear a fan softly humming somewhere in the distance. It sounded like it was coming from inside somewhere. A dim light snapped on at the foot of the casket, and a digital clock above the woman's head clicked on and counted down from two hours. It was then I recognized the woman in the casket. It was me. And I was thinking how much I wanted to see Cole one last time before I died."

The professor sat silently for a moment, concern written all over her face. "This can be tricky. We are dealing with the fact you are clairvoyant. We know you've seen occurrences by way of out-of-body experiences and visions. But your past experiences haven't shown us you have, as well, seen occurrences by way of dreams. And the thing we must consider is, just because you're clairvoyant doesn't mean you can't have symbolic dreams like people who aren't psychic."

"What do you mean by symbolic dreams?" Although Jenna already had a suspicion the professor was referring to the same type of dreams Barbara had mentioned to her this morning.

"When we experience circumstances in our lives that are worrisome, it can bring on symbolic dreams. A drastic change in your life could be the cause of it. A big decision you have to make, or different emotions over new or arising situations we find ourselves facing. All of these conditions are a recipe for symbolic dreams."

"But what could a dream about being buried alive mean?"

"Sometimes it is a sign that you either need to throw your old life away and begin a new one, or you are on the cusp of doing that. It could also mean you have so much on your plate that you are losing control."

The more Jenna considered this, the more sense it made. The upcoming wedding had caused more stress than she'd ever experienced. Although Cole thought he was doing the right thing by refusing to let her father pay for the wedding, it put more strain on their finances. In the end it didn't matter that he wholeheartedly wanted to help her plan every stage of the wedding, she felt solely responsible for the outcome. She'd have to admit her feeling like this wasn't his fault. She had been an independent person for so long. She suffered from the idea if things weren't single-handedly managed by her, they would not be done properly. And of course, she was on the cusp of a new life with Cole. With every day that passed, the last ten years spent building a life for herself slipped farther away. She realized it was not at all that she didn't want a life with Cole. She absolutely did. But deep down she feared losing her independence, and that had been all she'd had to hold on to for the last ten years.

"You look worried, Jenna. If you want to talk, I'm here. And you know this conversation won't go any further than these walls. I'm not Barbara."

She chuckled. It would be great to talk to someone not involved in her current situation. "I...It's just...I have this horrible habit of refusing help from others. The wedding has got me overly stressed. Cole wants to help, but I feel responsible for the planning. I worry about how full his plate is, so I find myself taking on the brunt of it and turning away his offers to help. I know I've done the same thing to Barbara."

The professor smiled, clasping her fingers together, as if she knew exactly where Jenna was coming from.

"I have a feeling you don't need my advice on what to do about that. I think you already know. It is perfectly okay to let other people share the reins. It's a learned behavior you've developed over the years causing you to deny other people the opportunity to help. And it is going to take a learned behavior to change it."

"Let me guess, you moonlight as a psychologist."

The professor laughed. "I have done some research on human behavior. It comes with the territory."

Fair enough. "I love Cole with all my heart. And I don't doubt he is my soulmate. I want nothing more than to be his wife. But it kind of feels like I'm giving up my independence too, ya know? I've had to rely on myself so long to take care of me and my daughter, I'm having a difficult time adjusting and sharing responsibility with someone else."

"I could tell you were a fiercely independent woman the first time I met you. Marrying Cole is not giving up your independence. It's only the acceptance of a partner with whom to experience life with and share the load. Of course, it's going to take some adjusting on behalf of both of you. But there is nothing worth having that doesn't. Barbara tells me you two were high-school sweethearts. And you've reunited after ten years. From the way she explained it, you guys have a love for one another most people search a lifetime for, but never find."

Even though Barbara and Cole had their differences, and rarely saw eye to eye, her best friend knew she and Cole were meant for each other. The professor was right. She wasn't giving up her independence but gaining the support of another for the rest of her life. "When you put it that way…"

"My father, rest his soul, used to tell me perception is in the eye of the beholder. It's the glass half empty, half full rule. I've lived my life by it, and it has never steered me wrong. Now, getting back to your dream. I think it's highly possible what you experienced is a symbolic dream, not a psychic vision. I've come to this conclusion because you are going through some drastic changes in your life right now. When we consider this, it's easy to conclude a symbolic dream is at the root of this."

"I just can't get over how vivid the whole thing was."

"Symbolic dreams are more vivid than most dreams. It doesn't surprise me it felt as real as you've described. The best way to combat them is to make a change in your life. But in your case, I can see it is you fighting the change that brought this dream on. So, I'd say embrace the change, and the dreams should stop."

"That easy, huh?"

"That depends on you. What does your instincts tell you about this change? Do you think you should accept it or fight it?"

"Marrying Cole? I think I should accept it. After all, it is what I want."

"Then stop fighting it."

It made perfect sense. Why couldn't she have seen this herself?

As Jenna thanked the professor, got up, and left the room, she couldn't believe how foolish she had been. Why was she inventing an issue where there wasn't one? Had she been such a worrywart if there hadn't been a worry to be found, she'd create one? She'd done this all her life, hadn't she?

Especially now, when she was finally on the verge of obtaining the one thing that would make her happiest, she had been working to thwart it. All because she believed nothing came without a price. That perhaps she didn't deserve a love such as Cole's. It was bullshit. A lie she'd fed herself so often she believed it.

But today had been the first day she'd seen it for what it was. A change in her life was coming, all right. It would start with the realization that sabotaging her happiness needed to stop. She'd come clean with Cole. Tell him about her fears and ask for his support. After all, when they reunited after ten years, they both made a promise they would never hide anything from each other ever again. If she expected him to live by that rule, she needed to as well.

Chapter Three

From the moment Jenna strolled through the door of Cole's house, the mouth-watering aroma of Italian food wafted in the air. Whistling resonated from the direction of the kitchen. She dropped her purse on the coffee table and followed the sound. She stood just inside the entrance, leaned against the casing, and studied Cole's movements as he shuffled from one end of the room to the other, gathering cooking utensils. He grabbed some spices from the rack and sprinkled them into a big pot simmering on the stove.

"I never realized cooking could be such a sexy undertaking," she said, then smiled when he spun around to face her.

A lopsided grin crept across his face. "You think I'm sexy, huh?"

"I was referring to the cooking."

"You were referring to the undertaking of the cooking."

"Okay, you win."

He drifted toward her, pinning her against the wall, then leaned in and whispered, "What did I win?"

She put her hand against his chest. "Not this time, hot rod. I'm starving and that smells too good to waste."

"Fine. I can wait until after dinner," he said, heading back toward the stove.

She followed, saying, "I can help. What do you want me to do?"

He peered back at her, his intense gaze sliding up one end of her body and down the other. "You can take off all your clothes and meet me in the bedroom." He winked and patted the countertop. "Or we can do it right here."

"I am not doing it on the countertop." She wandered over to the cabinet and got out two long-stemmed glasses, grabbed a bottle of Chardonnay out of the wine cooler, and poured them each a glass. She set his down on the counter, and then carried hers over to the table. "How did it go at the attorney's office?"

"Yeah, I wanted to talk to you about that. You're not going to believe this." He tasted the sauce, put the lid back in place, and turned the burner on under the pot of water. "My great-grandfather left us an inheritance of five million dollars."

Jenna spit out the wine. "He did what?"

"And that's not all. We are the owners of a three-hundred-acre ranch in Dallas with a twelve thousand square foot mansion."

"Oh, my God, Cole. You can't be serious."

"As a heart-attack." He pointed toward the manilla envelope sitting on the table and told her to open it.

After reading the letter his great-grandfather wrote, she gaped at him. "He left you the shares of his company too. Cole, I've heard of this company. Everybody has. I used to order Emily's toys from them all the time."

"I know. But I wanted to talk to you about selling off my shares."

"Why?"

"For a few reasons." After checking the sauce one more time, he turned the burner to low heat, and then sat down across from her. "Hershel didn't come about his wealth in an honorable way. He committed blackmail to acquire it."

"What do you mean?"

"His daughter, Jasmine, my grandmother, and the mother of Joseph and Derek was raped by a senator when she worked for him as an intern."

"That's terrible."

"That's how she got pregnant with the twin boys."

"That's why they were put up for adoption."

"Exactly. When Jasmine died a few years later, Hershel used the rape to blackmail the senator. He received a substantial amount of money to keep quiet about it. Then he used that money to invest in Toys Galore, making him a rich man."

"What kind of a father does that?"

"I was told by his attorney he was, let's just say, a very unpleasant man."

"The letter he wrote made it seem as if he regretted the ones he'd hurt in life. And he was sorry he never reached out to you. Is that why he left you with such a generous inheritance?"

"That's a good guess. I can't say for sure. But I don't agree with the things he's done, and because of that I feel it would be as equally wrong for me to accept the inheritance he left. That money was derived out of the pain my grandmother suffered. What happened to her had to have been devastating, and he capitalized on it. I can't excuse what he did."

"I don't think it's your place to. You didn't commit that wrong against her, he did."

"I know, but it feels like—"

"I think it would make it easier if you asked yourself if your grandmother had the opportunity to know you, would she want you to have this? If you were in her place, knowing your grandson was a good man, would you want him to keep this inheritance?"

"Yes. I would."

"Then it doesn't need to be any more complicated than that. But I want you to know no matter what you decide, I will stand by you."

The sentiment softened his eyes. "Thank you. That means a lot."

"Is this why you are considering selling off your shares of the company?"

"That has more to do with my brother, Dunston. Hershel didn't leave him as much as he did me. I can't help but feel it was unfair."

"Hershel explained in his letter he felt you were the more responsible one."

"He may be right, but I still feel my brother was cheated."

"Did your brother mention that?"

"He honestly didn't have much of a reaction to any of it."

"Are you thinking of selling your shares and splitting the money with Dunston?"

"That was my thought." He got up and tended to the sauce, adding the pasta to the boiling water. "I think it would be the right thing to do."

She stood from the table, wandered over to the counter, and sliced the bread, laying it out on a baking sheet, then headed to the fridge for the garlic butter. "If that's how you feel, I would encourage you to follow your heart."

He turned to her. "Yeah?"

"Yeah."

He stepped over to her and planted a kiss on her forehead, then took her into his arms. "Did I tell you how much I love you today?"

She giggled, wrestling away, getting on her tippy-toes, and kissing his lips. "I love you too, honey."

When he strode back to the stove, he said, "How do you feel about moving to Dallas?"

"Are you talking about the ranch you inherited?"

"I checked it out on one of those real estate sites. It's really something, Jenna. I think you'll fall in love with it."

Butterflies danced in her stomach at his words. "I'm not going to lie, it sounds heavenly. And I think Emily will love it, too."

"Oh, trust me. She will be in her glory."

He stirred the pasta as Jenna sauntered over and preheated the oven, preparing to bake the bread. "Perhaps we should take a day and go check it out."

"Absolutely. If we decide to go that route, it's a good thing I haven't heard back from the bank yet regarding the loan to build the ranch we discussed."

She set the table, as Cole drained the pasta. "See? It must be fate."

After sliding the bread into the oven, Cole refilled their wine glasses, and once she'd settled in at the table, he handed her a brochure, saying, "I found this in the mailbox today. I want you to call them."

Jenna stared at the colorful writing across the brochure. *Sara's Wedding Planning Services.* "Cole, I don't need—"

"Yes, you do. You won't let me help plan this wedding, and you've been going out of your mind doing it yourself."

"We can't afford it."

He glared at her. "You're kidding, right?"

She shook her head, remembering the inheritance. "I guess now we can, but the wedding is only a few weeks away and—"

"All the more reason for us to bring in reinforcements."

As she signaled opposition, she recalled the discussion she had with the professor today. It struck her those old habits of punishing herself unnecessarily were rearing their ugly head again. Truth be told, she needed the help. Admitting that and willing to share the reins with others was a step in the right direction. "Okay. I think it's a good idea."

"That was easier than I thought it would be," he remarked, stepping away to take the bread out of the oven.

Cole added the pasta to the sauce, tossed the bread into a wicker basket, and headed to the table with the food.

They filled their plates, and Jenna sat back, taking a sip of wine. "I wanted to talk to you about what happened at Professor Delaney's office today."

"I've been meaning to ask you about that."

"She felt strongly my episode was a symbolic dream, not a clairvoyant vision. And maybe she's right."

"Really?" His expression indicated surprise. "What did she say to convince you of that?"

"She explained she thought the dream was a

symbol of the change taking place in my life with our upcoming wedding, and how I was fighting it."

He frowned, and in his eyes was the question of why she would oppose their wedding.

"It's not what you think. It has to do with my fear of feeling like I was being forced to let go of my independence."

"I don't understand. Do you want to marry me, Jenna?"

"Oh, my God. More than you know. I promise it's not that at all."

"Then what is it?" He awaited her answer with questioning eyes.

"It's my own stubbornness. Over the years I've formed this habit of never believing what I thought was too good to be true. It's like, if anything good happened to me, I always had to question it, as if I just don't deserve to be happy."

"Do I make you happy?"

"You have been the only thing in my life, other than our daughter, that has made me truly happy. But a part of me was afraid it was too good to be true, and it couldn't last. And I think I was using the excuse that when we married, I would lose my independence as a way of distancing myself from the truth, which was, I'd eventually lose you."

She could tell he was getting frustrated. "Just tell me in English. What is it you're getting at?"

"You make me so happy, and I love you so much, I'm afraid of it."

He appeared incredulous. "You're afraid of me?"

"I'm afraid of how badly you could hurt me. How vulnerable I am when it comes to you."

"Oh my God, Jenna. That scares me too. I have spent so many years loving you. Even when you were gone. And now that you've come back into my life, believe me, I know how devastating the risk of losing you is. But having you with me, the hope of spending the rest of my life with you is worth every bit of the risk."

Relief washed over her to hear him say that. He was every bit as frightened as her. "I realize we will face hard times. We won't always agree with one another. And we will go through our own, personal hardships. I just hope we come through all that supporting one another. I hope we don't give up on each other, no matter what," she expressed.

"Jenna, I am one-hundred percent committed to this. I am devoted to loving you and seeing you through every hardship you could imagine facing now, when you're forty, and when you're ninety years old."

"I feel exactly the same way."

"Then we have nothing to fear, do we?" he said, sliding his hand over hers. "We only have everything to gain."

Incredible heat radiated from his hand, warming her soul. "I'm so glad I was able to talk to you about this."

"I'm always here for you. There is nothing you can't talk to me about."

"Thank you."

"We made a promise, remember? That we would never keep anything from each other ever again."

Her nod said she remembered. She slid a forkful of spaghetti into her mouth, chasing it down with a sip of wine. "This is really good."

"I told you I could cook," he said, digging in himself.

"So, when do I get to meet your brother?"

He dipped the wedge of bread into the sauce and took a bite. After swallowing, he said, "I was thinking about inviting him out to dinner tomorrow night. What do you think?"

"Barbara has been on my ass about us not spending enough time together. Maybe we can kill two birds with one stone."

"You're thinking of inviting Barbara out with us?"

"Why not?"

He shrugged, then took a sip of wine. "I think it's a good idea."

She stared at him incredulously. "Since when do you think inviting Barbara anywhere out with us is a good idea?" From the moment the suggestion left her lips, she figured she'd have an argument on her hands.

"She's your best friend, isn't she?"

"And your mortal enemy."

"C'mon. I can get along with Barbara."

"Yeah, when she's sleeping."

He took another bite, then said, "That's not true. We've been around each other before without getting into a single disagreement."

"When?"

"That time…just last week…" He groaned, defeated. "Never mind. You've made your point. So, what do you suggest, we avoid each other forever?"

"Just that you behave and play nice."

"I'm not the difficult one. She's so—"

"I know," she said, holding up her hand, suppressing a laugh at the childishness of his reaction.

"Well, she is."

This time, laughter burst from her.

Cole stared at her, a blank expression on his face. "What?"

"I swear, the two of you are the biggest children I know. You couldn't get along with each other if you were the last people on Earth."

"I'd throw myself off a cliff. Or I'd take a long swim in the ocean. Yeah, I could drown myself. That would be less painful then living in misery with Barbara."

She giggled uncontrollably.

"What, you find that funny?" He got up and approached her.

She couldn't stop laughing.

He said, "I say something about jumping off a cliff or drowning myself and you think it's hilarious."

If she supposed she could stop laughing before, she damn sure couldn't now.

"I'll show you funny," he said, leaning over and tickling her.

She jumped up from the chair, begging him to stop.

"Say uncle," he said.

She wrestled with him among fits of giggles as he continued his torment.

"Just say uncle and it will all be over."

"Uncle, uncle, uncle."

He stopped tickling her and she leaned against him, resting the back of her head on his shoulder, her ribcage hurting from laughing so much. Before she realized what hit her, the warmth of his lips was on her neck, unleashing a swirl of heated emotions spiraling through her. She inhaled deeply, doing her best to find her voice. "Do I need to say uncle again?"

Hoarse words reverberated in her ear. "I'm afraid that won't save you this time."

She twisted in his arms, surrendering to the lips that waited for her. It was a slow burning kiss that instantly caused a throbbing to develop between her legs.

His feathery kisses glided to her ear again. "I've been thinking about you all day, sweetheart."

Liquid heat shot through her at his confession. "What have you been thinking about doing to me?" she asked on pins and needles.

He unbuttoned the front of her dress and guided the material over her shoulders. Next, he unfastened her bra and tugged it down, revealing two firm breasts. As he stared at her body, the intensity in his eyes burned into her. "The thought of tasting you has driven me to insanity." His tongue circled around a swollen nipple while his hand cupped her other breast, massaging it slowly.

Jenna's breath caught, and she threw back her head. The anticipation for their love making had been building like an incredible wave since he cornered her inside his office earlier in the day. She'd wanted him then with a fervor that knew no bounds. The taste of his kiss and the touch of his hand had lingered, making it impossible for her to get beyond the image that formed in her mind of him bending her over his desk, tugging her panties down, and riding her from behind until a fierce orgasm rocked her body.

Now his hand ran down the length of her dress. He drew up the hem, and once he found the flesh of her inner thigh, the direction of his hand reversed course, trailing upward toward the hotness between her legs. His lips found the outside of her neck, and he wound his way to her earlobe, his teeth tugging on it gently. He whispered huskily, "I've been hard all day just thinking about touching you here."

Jenna braced herself for what was coming next. And when his fingers slid under her panties, stroking her clitoris, she closed her eyes, moaning with pleasure, and called out his name.

Cole stopped long enough to tug her panties down her hips and let them fall around her feet. She stepped out of them, and he propped her leg up on the chair she'd abandoned earlier. He knelt beneath her, and she waited, breath trapped in her chest.

The moment his tongue stroked her clitoris an explosion of pleasure erupted through her. She cried out with ecstasy as he lapped slowly, tortuously. Her fingers entwined in his hair, and she held on for dear life, afraid her legs would fold from the immense sexual gratification shooting through her.

Then he stood, picking her up, settled her legs around his hips, and carried her to the counter, setting her down. He slid her hand to the bulge in his pants and whispered against her ear, "Do you see how hard you make me? I've wanted to get inside you all damn day."

With a pounding heart, she unbuckled his belt, released the button of his jeans, and drew the zipper down. The moment her hand closed around his rock hard cock, he shuddered and let out a hoarse moan. "Oh, God, Jenna."

She didn't waste a minute, spreading her legs and guiding his silky shaft into the opening of her vagina.

His lips collided with hers as he drove himself deep

inside of her.

His slow, continuous thrusts sent an explosion of firebombs denotating throughout Jenna's body. She cried out, a series of loud moans erupting from her.

Then he drew himself out of her, staring into her eyes as if searching for something.

She swallowed hard, her voice throaty as she said, "What's wrong?"

He kissed her chin, dragging his lips down the slope of her throat, all the way to her breasts, where he stopped to suckle a nipple. He gazed at her again and said, "Do you want me, Jenna?"

Her skin still tingled where he'd fondled her just moments ago. "Don't play games."

He put his lips loosely against hers and demanded, "I want to hear you say it. Tell me you want me?"

His breath was hot against her, and her head swam with wanton desire for this man. The rise and fall of her chest were heavy and her heartbeat thumped in her ears. "I want you, Cole. If you make me wait, I think I'm going to die."

"Do you love me?"

She searched his expression, sensing his profound need to hear her say it. "I love you so much it hurts."

He stared at her with such intensity, it was as if he had opened his soul to her in that moment. He never took his eyes off her as he drove his cock into her again, causing her breath to catch.

"Oh, God, Cole. I want every inch of you, please. Don't stop."

"You feel so good, baby," he groaned, as he picked up the pace, riding her so fiercely her palms gripped the counter to keep from being thrust against the backsplash.

It was coming, and there was nothing she could do to hold it at bay. The first spasm shook Jenna, and she screamed out, her voice rising as her orgasm reached its peak.

Cole let loose, groaning as he thrust inside of her one last time. They clung to each other as the final shudder ripped through them.

When the dust settled, she looped her arms around his neck, touching her forehead to his. "I don't want you to ever question my love for you, Cole. I can't wait to be your wife. That will make me the happiest girl in the world."

He grinned into her eyes and responded, "I'm so glad to hear you say that. It's just the conversation we had tonight had me a little concerned. I want you to be sure this is what you want."

"Hey, I might not be sure of a lot of things in my life, but marrying you is the one thing I am sure of. Me and Emily need you."

"As long as there's a breath in me, you two ladies have got me, for better or worse."

"Thank you," she said, kissing him on the nose.

"I'm curious. What happened to, *I'm not doing it on the countertop?*"

A flush crept up her cheeks. "Hmm. Did I say that?"

"Yes, you did." He gripped the counter on either side of her, arms propping him up. He leaned in and kissed her until her head swam with dizziness.

When they resurfaced for air, he threatened, "And if you're not careful, soon to be wife, I'll take you on the countertop again."

Something told her it was going to be a long night.

****

Jenna held the phone against her ear as it rang. She stared at her second cup of coffee sitting on the kitchen table and figured it had become too cold to drink by now. It was probably a good thing. She'd already had enough thoughts running around her brain without the aid of too much caffeine making it worse.

"What are you doing?" Barbara asked, answering the phone.

"Wondering what you're up to today."

"Why?"

The brochure Cole handed her last night still lay on the table. Jenna picked it up and studied the colorful images. "Because I'm wondering if you'd like to accompany me to Sara's Wedding Planning Services."

Silence, and then, "You're hiring a wedding planner? Didn't you say you couldn't afford that?"

"That was before Cole's great grandfather left him an inheritance of five million dollars."

"What?"

"I know. I was as stunned as you."

"When in the hell did this happen?"

"He met with the trust attorney yesterday. Can you believe that?"

"I'm…just…oh, my God. That's great, Jenna! I'm so happy for you guys. Well, maybe not Cole."

"Barbara," she admonished.

Her friend laughed. "You know I'm kidding. Life wouldn't be near as fulfilling for me if I didn't have your fiancé to pick on. But I think it's wonderful. How exciting. Does this mean we get to plan the wedding of the century?"

"It means I can get a little help. Lord knows I need it desperately."

"What happened to Miss I can take care of it all myself?"

"She realized she couldn't. And Cole insisted."

"Oh, so, you'll listen to Mr. Know It All, but not your best friend when she tried to tell you the same thing."

"I'll have you know, Mr. Know It All has very effective measures of persuasion."

"Don't remind me. I haven't had a meaningful roll in the hay in so long I'm afraid the well has dried up."

"That reminds me. Me and Cole would like to know if you will accompany us to dinner tonight."

"Question. Why would the mention of my well drying up remind you to invite me to dinner with you and Cole? I don't know what you're thinking, but I don't swing that way, and I'm not that desperate…yet. But you might try checking back with me in another month."

Jenna laughed. "Cole is inviting his brother, Dunston to dinner."

"Since when does he have a brother?"

"He just found out about him yesterday."

"So, you think Cole's brother has some association with the condition of my well."

"He could."

"Have you met him?"

"Not yet."

"Then what makes you think I'd want him to water my well?"

"Because you said yourself your well needs watering."

"That doesn't mean I'd let just anyone water it. The guy could be as unsightly as a warthog."

"He's Cole's brother."

"Does he act like him?"

"I don't know. Geez."

"Is he married?"

"I didn't think to ask."

"Some fine match-maker you are."

"It's not like I planned this. The thought just occurred to me."

"I'll go to dinner with you guys. But not because I'm willing to be a guinea pig in this new matchmaking endeavor you've taken on, but because I'm curious what a second version of Cole would act and look like. God help me. I'm sure I'm in for a real treat."

"So, can you go with me today?"

"I thought you had work this morning?"

"I called my manager. She can handle things at the office by herself for one day. I can wait until you get off work to go if you need me to."

"Screw it. They owe me a few vacation days anyhow. Why don't you pick me up? We'll ride together."

"Okay. Let me jump in the shower and I'll be on my way in about an hour."

"See you then."

Jenna got off the phone, set it on the table, and threw her attention back into reading the brochure. *Walk ins welcome.* Thank God. She was not only a walk in. She was a walking disaster.

Chapter Four

The office of Sara's Wedding Planning Services was housed in a charming Victorian style home in the heart of downtown McKinney. Not a mile up the road sat the historic McKinney square. Jenna remembered taking many trips through the square when she was a kid, as her mother loved to browse the many antique shops.

As Jenna and Barb moseyed along the brick path leading up to the home, her friend couldn't contain her excitement. "This is going to be so much fun," Barbara said, peering back at her with adventure in her eyes. "I always wanted to help plan a wedding."

Although Jenna shared her enthusiasm for the planning of the upcoming nuptials, the most prominent emotion running through her was relief she'd finally get the help she needed to pull this together. Cole had been right. She had bitten off more than she could chew by stubbornly insisting she could manage it all by herself.

"I'm really glad you decided to do this," Barbara said, as they approached the door.

Jenna nodded her agreement, and they strode in together.

The young woman sitting behind the desk close to the entrance peered up and smiled warmly. "Good morning, ladies. What can I help you with?"

Jenna stepped toward the desk and laid the

brochure down in front of her. "I'd like to inquire about your wedding planning services."

The lady's expressive, brown eyes scanned the brochure. Then she picked it up, studying it with bewilderment. "If you don't mind me asking, where did you get this?"

"It came in the mail."

"Hmm." She read through the pamphlet, appearing no less perplexed for her trouble. "That's strange. Although we've done different types of advertising over the years, mailing brochures has never been one of them."

Jenna was lost for words. But before she could react, the woman shrugged, saying, "Perhaps the PR department is trying something new and didn't tell me."

"So, you're taking walk ins, right?" Jenna asked, worried the lady was going to turn her away. After all the convincing it had taken for her to finally reach out for help, now that she realized how desperately she needed it, the fear she wouldn't get it was terrifying, especially this close to the date of the wedding.

The girl peered around the mostly empty room, her attention settling on the only couple lounging in the high-back chairs a good thirty feet away. "I think Amy is taking care of them," she said, gesturing toward the man and woman. "But let me check with Sylvia to see how her schedule looks today." She stood and excused herself.

As the woman turned the corner, Barbara eyed Jenna, frowning. "Do these people know what they're doing?"

"I'm not sure. But you'd think the staff would be privy to their advertising strategies."

"It's just weird," Barb speculated.

The woman came strolling back, beaming as if she'd just solved the world's problems. "Sylvia is busy today, but we have a wedding planner open to see you ladies. She's a new hire but has lots of experience."

Jenna couldn't help but wonder why her comment came off as more of an attempt to convince them the wedding planner she mentioned was suitable for the job, instead of talented at it.

"If you'll follow me," the woman said, "I'll show you to her office."

With an air of uncertainty, Jenna followed close behind Barbara down a long hallway, until approaching a suite at the end. If her hesitancy hadn't heightened during the trek to the wedding planner's office, it did when she caught a glimpse of the person sitting behind the desk.

Ava's jaw dropped the second their attention collided. Cole's ex-lover glanced away and cleared her throat, struggling to pull herself together. She appeared every bit as stunned as Jenna.

Finally, the nice lady who escorted her and Barbara to the suite spoke up. "Ladies, this is Ms. Kingsley. She'll oversee planning your wedding."

At the woman's prompting, Ava gathered her senses, stood, straightened, and stepped from behind her desk, putting her hand out to Jenna.

Jenna noticed her hand was shaking, and her smile wasn't nearly the showy spectacle it had been when she'd interrupted her and Cole at lunch yesterday. Was that warmth radiating from the woman's eyes? Either way it was too little too late.

"I think there's been a huge mistake," Jenna said,

her attention wandering toward the lady who had showed them in. "My apologies." She marched to the door, and then peered back at the woman one last time. "I didn't mean to waste your time."

As Jenna headed down the hall, footsteps plodded behind her. Barbara caught up with her quickly. "What was that all about?"

"Nothing," she answered, never breaking her stride.

"Nothing, my ass."

Jenna thrust the door open and headed straight for her car. "It's nothing."

"Bullshit. How do you know that woman?"

"She's just someone Cole knows."

After they approached the car and Jenna went for the door handle, Barbara covered it with her hand. "We're not leaving until you start talking."

"Get out of my way, Barbara." If expressions could kill, her friend would have dropped dead.

Barbara wasn't deterred. "You'll have to pry my cold, dead hand from this handle. Just tell me who the hell she is already."

"It's none of your business!" Jenna angrily grabbed for the door handle, and a struggle ensued.

But Barb's grip wasn't budging. "Look. You're my best friend, and I could see how upset seeing her made you. That makes it my business."

"Is nothing off limits to you?" Jenna complained, digging in harder to get control of the door handle.

"You act like she slept with Cole or something."

Jenna let go of the handle, staring at her friend as if her intense gaze had the power to peel away the layers of her face like an onion.

"Oh my God, that's it, isn't it?"

"She's an ex-girlfriend since you have to know."

"It was a long time ago," someone said from behind.

Jenna peered over her shoulder to find Ava standing there, an expression of misery etched into her face.

"How long have you been standing there eavesdropping," Jenna asked between gritted teeth.

Ava lowered her head. "I came out to apologize for my atrocious behavior the other day at the restaurant. I know there's no excuse for the way I acted."

"You got that right," Jenna remarked with disdain, turning to fling the car door open.

"What happened at the restaurant?" Barb cut in.

"I'm sure Ava here will be happy to explain that," Jenna offered, placing her hands on her hips.

"This is between you and me, Jenna," Ava said, a flush in her cheeks, and a slight tone of annoyance in her voice.

"Let's get one thing straight," Jenna shot back, anger pumping through her veins with the force of a fire hydrant. "There is no you and me, there's just you who rudely interrupted me and my fiancé while we were having lunch to fawn all over him in front of me and act like a complete bitch. Does that sound about right?"

To Jenna's surprise, the irritated expression melted off her face. She averted her eyes, peered off into the distance, and whispered, "You're right. I can't believe I did that."

"Then why did you do it?" Jenna wanted to know, still fuming.

The woman met her heated gaze. "The truth is I did

it because I was jealous. The whole time me and Cole dated, I was the one who wanted a serious relationship. Every time I tried to get close, he would distance himself. I always thought it was me. I must have been the one doing something wrong. But seeing him with you yesterday, and the loving way he looked at you, I realized, after all this time, it wasn't me at all. It had been you all along. You stole his heart, and he never got over you. It wasn't anyone's fault. It's just the way love works. He couldn't give me what he didn't have to give." She peered down and shook her head. "It really set in on me after I left the restaurant. The more I thought about it, the more sense it made, why he acted the way he did when we were together. And to be honest, seeing what I witnessed between the two of you made it possible for me to finally move on. Then I felt badly for the way I treated you. It wasn't fair. And I sincerely hope you will accept my apology."

Jenna was floored. Of all the words she would have expected to tumble out of Ava's mouth, that spiel wasn't one of them. Now guilt set in for the way she'd laid into her moments ago. But in all honesty, she did have it coming. Jenna sighed, realizing she may have judged her too harshly and said, "I accept your apology." Cole was certainly a catch, and she couldn't blame the woman for wanting to hold on to him back then.

A hint of a smile played across Ava's lips. "I'm so glad to hear you say that. And I'm thankful to have had this opportunity to express myself. I'd like very much to start over if that's okay. And I would be honored to plan yours and Cole's wedding if you'll give me that chance."

"I don't know," Jenna said, shaking her head. "I'm not sure how Cole would feel about that."

"I understand," Ava said, appearing regretful. "I hope you'll consider talking this over with him. The least I can do is try to make amends for what I've done. Here's my business card if you decide to move forward with me as your wedding planner. And if you do, I promise I will do everything in my power to make sure you have the perfect wedding."

Jenna took the card and issued a pleasant goodbye before she and Barbara climbed into the car. As Ava headed back inside, Barbara piped up. "You're seriously not considering hiring that girl, are you?"

"I don't know.'

"What?"

She peered over at Barb as she turned the key in the ignition. "You think I can't handle hiring Cole's ex as our wedding planner?"

"Why would you want to?"

Jenna glanced in the rearview mirror as she backed out of the driveway. "Maybe I want to prove a point to my fiancé that I'm secure in our relationship."

"Is there a reason Cole wouldn't know that?"

"I said a few things last night. I think he took it the wrong way, and now he's worried I might not be ready to make this commitment. But I am."

"And hiring his ex-lover to plan your wedding will convince him of that how, exactly?"

Jenna stopped the car, shifted to drive, and stared at Barbara. "Because if hiring his ex to plan our wedding doesn't bother me, then obviously I'm confident enough in our relationship that I feel no one or nothing can come between us."

"So, do you?"

"Do I what?" Jenna asked, heading toward the street and pausing to yield to traffic.

"Feel that confident."

"Yes. But I need to convince Cole of that."

As Jenna headed out on Virginia Parkway, Barbara said, "I can think of only a hundred different ways this could blow up in your face."

"Now you don't have confidence in me either."

"It's not you I lack confidence in. It's her."

"I think she sincerely feels badly for the way she acted. And I think she wants to make amends. Don't you?"

"That's not the point. Can you trust her?"

"I don't know. But I think everyone deserves a second chance."

"Are you willing to wager your wedding on it?"

"I'm a big enough person to forgive her. Sometimes all a person needs are the opportunity to prove they are worthy of it. If she does anything to make me regret that decision, I'll call it off and hire someone else."

"How do you know Cole will go for this?"

"I don't."

****

At twelve o'clock Cole sat behind his desk at the precinct and bit into a turkey sandwich as he reflected on the phone conversation he just had with Sebastian Sawyer, the thirty percent shareholder of the toy company Cole inherited. And as Hershel had warned, the man tried to swindle him the moment he had been told Cole wanted to sell his shares of the company. The man made it sound as if Toys Galore wasn't worth the amount of money Cole already knew it was by having done extensive research for half of the morning. He may not have been as business savvy as his great-grandfather, but he was no idiot either. And he wasn't about to let some fast-talking swindlers take him for a ride.

As soon as he finished off the last bite, he crumpled the sandwich wrapper, tossed it into the trash, and then picked up his cell phone, dialing an old friend's number.

After Dario Vazquez answered, Cole said, "Hey, man, I'm in a bit of a predicament and I need your help."

"Sure. Whatever I can do."

"I inherited five million dollars from my grandfather, and he also left me his shares of the company he owned, Toys Galore."

"That's one of the biggest toy distributors out there. Congratulations, man. That's great news."

Cole figured since Dario had handled the affairs surrounding his wife Suzy's inheritance of the oil company her father left her when he passed away, he'd have enough experience to offer some guidance. "I've decided to sell off the shares, and I was hoping to get their full worth. The problem is, I'm not at all sure what I'm doing here. What do you suggest?"

"You said shares. How many other shareholders are we talking?"

"Me and two others. I own sixty percent, one of the others owns thirty, and the third owns ten."

"And you're wanting to sell your shares to one of the other shareholders?"

"For the sake of convenience and to save myself

the hassle of a long, drawn-out process, that would be nice."

"Let me guess, you've been briefed on the fact the company is not worth that much on paper."

Cole grinned, throwing his boots up on the desk. There was no doubt he'd turned to the right man. "That is exactly what I've been told."

Dario laughed. "Of course, it is. I'm assuming you didn't make a deal."

"Hell no. I wasn't born yesterday."

"Good. I'm going to put you in touch with a badass corporate lawyer I used when Suzy went through that nightmare with the shareholders of the oil company she inherited from Fred. This guy knows his shit and doesn't play games. His name is Angelo Berlusconi, originally from the Bronx with family ties to the Italian mafia. He's done some knuckle-cracking stuff in his day. He's smart and he's got a lot of muscle in the legal circles."

"Do you have his number?"

"I'll have to call him first. He won't talk to you if he doesn't know who you are."

"I have a meeting with these other shareholders in a few hours."

"What time is the meeting?"

"Three o'clock."

"Okay. Let me give him a ring. If he's not in court, he'll answer my call. I'll let him know it's urgent."

Cole rubbed the back of his neck, feeling the time crunch he was under. "Don't leave me hanging, Dario."

"Don't worry, brother. He'll call before your meeting."

"Okay, man. Thanks for your help."

"Anytime."

As Cole ended the call with his buddy, pushing his concern to the back of his mind for now, his phone rang. This time it was Jenna. A warm emotion fluttered through him causing a smile to surface for the first time today. He'd scarcely been able to get their fiery love making from last night out of his mind. He wondered if there would ever come a day he'd be able to keep his hands off her. He couldn't imagine that ever happening. "Hey, babe. I was just thinking about you."

"Oh yeah? I've been thinking about you too."

"Have you been thinking about doing to me what you did to me last night?" He was overcome with a heart pounding thrill waiting for her answer. It was almost scary how much influence she had over his happiness.

"Oh, you want a repeat, do you?"

"I'd absolutely love one. Are you offering?"

"I fear we're going to drop dead from sex."

He chuckled. "So, how'd it go at the wedding planners?"

"Quite interesting. And it's why I'm calling. You're not going to believe who works there."

Cole drew a blank. "I give."

"Ava Kingsley."

"You're kidding." Disappointment settled over him. "I'm sorry, sweetheart. I'm sure she's the last person you wanted to see. Now I feel badly for recommending you go there." He wanted to kick himself for making such a huge mistake, especially since it had taken so long to convince Jenna to accept help. "Don't worry. I'm sure there are plenty of wedding planning services to choose from."

"It's okay, Cole. Surprisingly, she was very apologetic and kind."

"What do you mean?" That certainly did not describe her attitude yesterday. The woman was brazenly rude and the whole ordeal had made him uncomfortable as hell.

"She came out and apologized to me. Explained she had been sore over losing you because she blamed herself. She told me she didn't realize I was the reason you couldn't ever commit to her. But then she saw us together and realized how much you loved me, and it became clear that was the reason why the relationship you two had together couldn't work. She even told me seeing us together helped to give her closure."

He didn't know what to think of that. But for the time he'd known Ava, she'd never shown such a jealous and unpleasant side as she had at the restaurant yesterday. And he had to admit, it shocked him she would act that way.

"As strange as it is for me to say this, I think she meant it."

At least he was relieved their surprise meeting hadn't gone badly. After the heated exchange he'd witnessed between the two ladies yesterday, he could imagine a scene with major hair pulling and flying desk chairs. "I'm glad she felt remorse for the way she treated you. You didn't deserve that."

"That's what she said."

"And she's right about that. You know, I never realized the break-up affected her that way."

"Who can blame her. Getting over you isn't an easy thing. I failed miserably at it."

That was one failure of Jenna's he thanked God for

every day. "I'm happy to know she's put it to rest. What do you say we do a little research this evening to find another wedding planner?"

"Here's the thing. Ava wanted me to talk to you about it, and if you're comfortable with it, she would still like to help us plan the wedding."

This conversation just kept getting interesting. "Uh, are you two best friends now or something? Because I'm not sure I can handle that."

Jenna laughed. "It's just I could tell she felt really badly about what happened. And she wants to make it up to us."

"It isn't about what she wants, Jenna. It's about what you want."

"That's not true. It's about what *we* want."

"Listen, I'm a guy, sweetheart. All it takes to make me happy is a six-pack of beer and a football game. But if you accept her help with this, I want to make sure you're making that decision based on your satisfaction, not hers. What if you regret letting Ava do this?"

"I've decided to give it a few days. See what she can come up with. If I'm not happy, I'll hire someone else. I know the wedding is only a few weeks away, but I can spare a few days. She might work extra hard for us because she is trying to make amends."

"Why do you want to hire her when you can have your pick of anyone?"

Jenna sighed. After a few minutes, she said, "I've been giving this a lot of thought, and I think maybe it was fate we got that particular brochure in the mailbox. I believe the right thing to do is forgive her. I feel like everyone deserves a second chance like we were given. But I won't commit to this if you're uncomfortable with it."

"I have no feelings for Ava one way or the other. My focus and concern are with you, honey. If you feel strongly in your heart this is the right thing to do, then I'm all for it."

"Are you sure, Cole?"

"Yes, ma'am."

"Then it's settled. I'll give her a call and let her know of our decision. Did you have your business meeting yet?"

"It's set for three o'clock, remember? I figure while I'm waiting, I'll drop by the inn to see Dunston and invite him to dinner tonight."

"Emily is supposed to call us when they get back from Disneyland. I hope she's enjoying her summer vacation with my parents."

Although Cole missed his nine-year-old daughter, she needed to spend some time with her grandparents. The Langleys had waited five months to see her. "I know. I can't wait to talk to her."

As Jenna told him goodbye, and he set the phone on his desk, he couldn't help but wonder if she had made the right call with Ava. The woman had seemed to be warm and affectionate back when they were dating. In fact, when he broke it off with her, she'd acted like she half expected it. That was why the foul behavior she'd displayed in the restaurant had thrown him for a loop. Perhaps Jenna was right, and she'd always felt as if she'd done something to cause him to break it off with her. If that was the case, he was glad she now realized the truth. His inability to commit to relationships never had anything to do with Ava, or any of the other women he'd carried on with for a short time. It was always Jenna. No matter what happened over the years, her memory refused to let him move on with someone else. And now he had no doubt it was because they were meant to find each other once again.

As he rose from his chair, grabbed his keys, and headed for the door, he decided he ought to trust Jenna's judgement where it concerned Ava. His fiancée's intuition had been spot-on many times before. After all, he'd learned that lesson through dealing with his father's murders, and how she'd had visions of the killings. And he had to admire her willingness to forgive. It was certainly something that she'd had the gumption to hire his ex-girlfriend to plan their wedding. And it spoke volumes to how much she trusted him, and how secure she must be in their relationship.

Making his way across the parking lot he had to stop and ask himself why then, was there this uneasiness in his gut. He pushed the emotion aside as he climbed in his truck and started the engine. The best thing to do would be to rely on Jenna's judgement. Besides, there was a tone of tranquility in her voice he hadn't heard in months. She was finally relaxing, and if she seemed at peace with this decision, he didn't want to be the one to upset the apple cart.

****

Cole swung his truck into the entrance of the McKinney Inn just as his phone rang. He quickly found a parking spot and slid his finger across the screen answering the call. "Detective Rainwater."

"Detective, this is Angelo Berlusconi. Dario called me on your behalf. How much negotiation has taken place for the sale of your shares with the company shareholders?"

The man got right to the point. Cole found the approach refreshing. "None. I've done a little research and have a suspicion Toys Galore is worth quite a bit more than what I'm being told."

"You bet it is. With your permission, I'd like to fax these profit and loss sheets over to Sebastian Sawyer before the meeting. Let him stew on those while he's waiting for us to arrive."

"Are you telling me you managed to get your hands on the company's profit and loss sheets?" Cole could not believe what he was hearing. The release of those documents would have only been made possible by the approval of someone on the company's board who had the authority to make such a decision.

"I hope that's okay with you. I knew we didn't have much time. So, I took the liberty."

"I don't understand. Wouldn't you have needed to get approval from someone on the company's board to get financial records? The shareholders will be in negotiations with me. I can't imagine they would have offered up that information."

"You are on the company's board, Mr. Rainwater. Remember, you inherited shares of the company."

Cole's mouth dropped open. Why hadn't he considered that himself? As sixty percent owner of Toys Galore, he had access to just as much of the financials as the other shareholders did.

"Like I said, I knew we were crunched for time, so as your counsel I got straight to work. I will need you to sign some documents though."

No doubt documents he should have signed before Berlusconi was able to get his hands on the financial reports. The guy was resourceful. He'd give him that.

"All right. Bring them with you to the meeting and I'll sign them."

"Great. I'll handle everything else. Your shares are worth one-hundred-million, Mr. Rainwater."

"You can't be serious?" Cole considered pinching himself. He must be dreaming.

"My fee is twenty-five percent."

"That's a bit high, isn't it?"

"Take it or leave it. No other attorney can get you half that much for your shares. But me and Sabastian Sawyer go way back. Let's just say he owes me. I'll get you every penny. You have my word."

"Okay, Mr. Berlusconi. I'll see you at three."

"See you then, Mr. Rainwater."

Cole wandered across the parking lot, took the hotel elevator to the second floor, and trekked down the long, narrow corridor to his brother's room in a trance-like state. How had events in his life transpired so dramatically over the past few days? It all started with the discovery his great-grandfather left him an inheritance. He'd been hopping from one roller coaster to another ever since. He kept waiting for the slow-down, but it hadn't happened yet. With the way things were going, he wondered if it ever would.

He knocked on Dunston's door and waited at least three minutes before it swung open. The man stood there barefoot, in a pair of jeans and no shirt. His disheveled hair told Cole he'd roused him out of bed. "Sorry. I didn't mean to wake you."

Dunston rubbed the back of his neck and yawned. "It's okay. I needed to get up anyway." He left the door standing open as he wandered back into the room.

Cole took it as an invitation and stepped inside,

closing the door behind him. By the appearance of the place, a suitcase lying open on the floor with clothes spilling out, an empty pizza box, and a few crushed beer cans and Styrofoam cups littering the table, he figured tidiness was not his brother's strong suit.

Dunston grabbed a shirt strewn over the back of the only chair in the room and tugged it over his head. Then he sat down, yawned again, and grabbed a pair of sandals.

The only light in the place glimmered from a small sconce on the wall close to the headboard. Cole stepped over to the drapes and peered back at his brother before pulling them open. "Do you mind?"

He nodded. "Go ahead. What time is it?"

Cole checked his watch after drawing open the drapes. "A little past two."

"Damn. I'm glad you stopped by. I might have slept the day away."

"Late night?"

"I went to Arlington last night and checked out the new pad good ol' Grandpa left me. I didn't get back until after two in the morning."

Cole wandered over to the small desk and leaned against it. Crossing his legs out in front of him. "So, how was it?"

Dunston gave a lopsided grin. "I'm not used to owning anything so nice. Dear Mom was a strictly necessities kind of gal. One pair of new shoes at the beginning of the school year, and hand-me-down clothes from the corner thrift store, while she spent the rest of her money on booze in between times she was lucky enough to stumble across a sugar daddy. He was usually some low-life asshole who couldn't resist slapping me around. You know, making a man of me."

Cole glanced down and shook his head. "Man, I'm sorry you had to live through that shit. It couldn't have been easy."

"Nah, I had a few good friends. Let's just say I spent a lot of time away from home."

With what he, himself went through as a teenager because of what his father had done, Cole realized from experience tragic events like that either made you stronger or weaker. And Dunston's carefree attitude concerning the trials he'd faced in life told Cole he and his brother were a lot alike in the sense they'd used their negative experiences to grow and become stronger. That was a commendable thing. "I'm glad to have discovered you exist."

"I hear ya, bro. It's nice to know I have a brother in this crazy world."

"Me and Jenna would like to know if you'd care to join us for dinner tonight."

"She your girl?"

"Yep. We're getting married in a few weeks. She's amazing. I think you'll really like her."

"She must be something to put up with a Rainwater, right?"

Cole chuckled. "I suppose you're right about that."

"Sure, man. I can't wait to meet her."

"How about six o'clock at Hank's Steakhouse? Do you need the address?"

Dunston grinned. "You know, nowadays all you have to do is speak the name of a business into your phone, and wham, the address pops up just like that. It'll even tell you how to get there. It's incredible."

Cole nodded with a smirk. "Okay, smartass. I'll see

you tonight then."

He showed himself out, realizing he was looking forward to dinner more now than he had before stopping by to see Dunston. He was becoming fond of his younger brother. The guy reminded him a lot of himself.

On second thought, was that a good thing?

Chapter Five

Once inside the massive skyscraper that was Toys Galore in downtown Dallas, Cole rode the elevator to the boardroom on the seventeenth floor.

The doors slid open with a ding, and he hesitated before stepping off the car. Nerves tightened like a fist in his gut. He was certainly out of his element on this, and quite outnumbered. Behind the door down the hall would be two shareholders circling like sharks in blood-soaked water waiting to feed. Compliments of the Internet, he'd learned as much about the businessmen as search engines would allow. He could picture the face of sixty-eight-year-old Wyatt Hendrix, ten percent shareholder, white, thinning hair, trimmed mustache, and the sharp, dark eyes of a crow. He was a family man, owned a ranch and a vacation home in Maui. His net worth was a little over two-hundred million.

The younger of the shareholders was Sebastian Sawyer at thirty-eight years old. Sandy, brown hair, a pretty-boy smile, and a movie star twinkle in his blue eyes. His net worth was undisclosed. He owned thirty percent of Toys Galore and was a shrewd businessman according to Cole's discovery.

As he trudged down the hall, advancing toward suite seventeen, he hoped Angelo Berlusconi lived up to his reputation. The guy was certainly taking a big enough chunk of the sale.

He put his hand on the doorknob, took a deep breath, and stepped inside.

The three men sitting around the long, oval table, glanced up at the disturbance. One of them didn't resemble the images he'd studied online, so it was a good indication the man getting to his feet and coming toward him was his attorney.

"Ahh, here's the man," Berlusconi announced, clapping Cole on the back, and showing him to a seat next to the chair he had been sitting in.

As Cole sat down, Wyatt grumbled an acknowledgment of his presence, while a poor attempt at a grin fleetingly skittered across Sebastian's face, and he said, "Mr. Rainwater, it's nice to finally make your acquaintance." Judging by the downtrodden expressions on the shareholders' faces, it was highly likely Mr. Sawyer's statement didn't have a grain of truth in it. Then Wyatt turned to Sebastian and said, "He favors the old man, doesn't he?"

For all Cole's research, he hadn't run across a single picture of his great-grandfather. But then again, he was too busy scouring the Internet rounding up as much information on the two of them before their meeting today to be concerned with Hershel.

Sebastian's attention floated toward a series of pictures on the wall opposite him. Three men in business suits posed for the camera. The two on the end were of both shareholders in the room. The one in the middle had to be Hershel. Even if Cole wouldn't have guessed that by recognizing the other men in the picture, and assuming the third one had to be his great-grandfather, he would have known it by the familiar traits of the man in the picture. The gray eyes, and the cleft chin some of the Rainwater men acquired. Although he was a handsome man, even at the ripe age he must have been when the picture was taken, there existed a hardness in his eyes that instantly reaffirmed the rumors of Hershel's ruthless behavior must be true.

Berlusconi spoke up. "Mr. Rainwater, the man on your right is Wyatt Hendrix, and the other is—"

"Oh, cut the crap!" Wyatt burst out, anger seething just below the collected demeanor the man appeared to be holding on to by a thread. "You have your purchase agreement. We signed the bloody thing. You could have given it to your client. We have better things to do than participate in this Godforsaken circus of yours."

Sebastian glanced down, appearing as beaten as Cole had ever seen someone.

"I wouldn't call discussing a fair purchase price a circus," Berlusconi said.

"Fair, my ass!" Wyatt lunged out of the chair. He put his hands on the glass table, and leaned across it, eyes narrowing like a laser. "All you've done is throw your weight around." He turned to the other shareholder. "Isn't that right, Sebastian?"

Mr. Sawyer wouldn't dare avert his gaze away from the table. He said in a small voice, "Let's just get this over with."

Cole couldn't be sure exactly what had taken place before he arrived here, but he had a good suspicion it had everything to do with the statement his attorney made over the phone earlier in the day, *Sebastian owes me*.

"I haven't asked a penny more than what my client's shares are worth, and you damn well know that," Berlusconi said.

Wyatt became even more unhinged. "This wasn't a negotiation! It was blackmail!"

Berlusconi collectively abandoned his chair, matching the man's furious stare. "We all have our skeletons in the closet, don't we, Mr. Hendrix?"

"You son-of-a-bitch!" A murderous glower emanated from Wyatt's eyes.

Berlusconi grinned derisively. "It's about time you caught on. We're not kids playing in a sandbox. My client deserves fair market value for his shares. And I will get that for him using any means necessary. Being the unscrupulous businessman you are, it's disappointing this would be so surprising to you. But then again, it's not, is it? Only when the tables are turned. Something tells me you're not accustomed to that. The world is full of wolves, Mr. Hendrix. Some are better hunters than you. The way I see it, you are the last person to talk to me about blackmail."

As the two men continued to stare each other down, Wyatt finally relented, glancing away. He opened his briefcase, shoving papers inside, saying, "I signed your damn agreement. I'm not sticking around for this horseshow." He headed toward the door and stopped as he approached it. Cole could see burning defeat in the man's eyes as he stared dead at him. "Out of all the attorneys out there," Mr. Hendrix said, "I don't know how you managed to stumble across him. But I guess congratulations are in order. I don't ever want to see either one of you again." The man stepped out of the room, shutting the door so hard it rattled in its frame.

After the three men finished up business in the boardroom, Cole couldn't help asking Berlusconi as he walked with him through the parking lot, "So, what exactly did you have on Sebastian Sawyer anyhow?"

The man grinned. "Back when I got my license, I started out as a defense attorney. Sebastian's case was one of the first I handled. I did it *pro bono* because I knew the circles he ran in, and I realized someday I may need to call in a favor from such a bare-knuckled businessman as Sawyer. The agreement was, if I won him the case, he'd owe me. When I came to collect on the favor, he'd pay up, no matter what the circumstances were. I won the case, and this was the favor."

"What case was that if you don't mind me asking?"

"Attorney/client privilege, my friend. Let's just say the Pied Piper came calling and he was facing some major prison time. But when I finished with the case, he was a free man. I took a lot of *pro bono* cases at that time, and I collected a lot of favors. That was my recipe to success, Mr. Rainwater."

Cole had to admire the guy. He seemed to make it work for him, even if some of his tactics seemed on the brass-knuckle side. The world was not a fair playground, and it sometimes called for a harsher approach for those who desired to be successful in it. It appeared this was precisely the way Berlusconi clawed his way to the top.

After issuing his goodbyes to the attorney, Cole hopped in his truck and picked up the phone to call Jenna. When she answered, he laid out the details of what transpired in the boardroom.

****

Barbara rode with Jenna and Cole to Hank's Steakhouse. They arrived five minutes earlier than the agreed upon time. As Cole stepped from the driver's side of Jenna's car, he spotted Dunston's older model vehicle parked three spaces down from theirs. He'd taken notice of the ill-repair of the automobile when he had watched his brother climb into it when they'd left from the meeting with the trust attorney yesterday. The generous inheritance they'd received would drastically alter the life of the guy, Cole guessed right off the bat, who had less than the average Joe most, if not all, his life. It was a curious thought how well Dunston would adjust to such a change. But then it was hard to weight the outcome of that when he had his hands full dealing with his own unexpected windfall.

When they checked in with the hostess, and Cole gave his name, the young woman smiled expectantly and led them to a table where Dunston sat alone waiting for them. It was apparent right away his brother had taken extra care with his appearance tonight. His choice of clothes was sharp. A tie, brown corduroy jacket, and dark, pressed jeans with a pair of loafers. His hair was combed back, showing off the receding hairline that added to his brother's good looks.

Dunston nodded a greeting and stood, plucking out a chair for Barbara the same time Cole drew one out for his fiancée.

As they all settled in, Barbara broke the silence, giving Dunston a once over and declaring, "God, you're hot."

Her unexpected words left everyone speechless, until Dunston laughed and said, "That's the kind of honesty a man can appreciate. Who are you, by the way?"

"My name is Barbara. But I'll let you call me

Barb."

Dunston gave an intriguing grin. "Okay, Barb. Cole didn't mention a third person coming tonight. Not that I'm complaining."

"Doesn't surprise me," Barbara quipped. "Cole doesn't really like me. I'm shocked he agreed to let me come."

Jenna's eyes floated toward the ceiling, and she said, "God, Barbara. Why are you so—"

"Honest?" her friend finished for her. "You know it's true."

"It certainly is not," Jenna argued.

"Oh, it is," Cole put in.

"See?" Barbara said, stabbing out a hand to prove her point. "It's not like I care what he thinks anyhow. I never have."

"You'll have to excuse these two," Jenna said to Dunston. "They've been like this with each other since we were teenagers."

"Cole has a problem with people who speak their mind," Barb said, putting in her two cents.

"I have a problem with people who act like morons and say stupid shit," Cole corrected.

"Stop it, right now," Jenna warned them both. "And I mean it."

"Yes, mother dear," Barbara smarted off.

Jenna smiled, despite her obvious annoyance. She said to Dunston, "Barbara has been my best friend since high school."

"Oh," Dunston said, an expression of understanding crossing his face. "And I guess you three grew up together."

"Me and Cole reunited when I came back to Texas

after being gone for ten years. That's when I met up with Barb again." Her expression appeared dismissive. "It's a long story."

A server headed in their direction, and a huge wave of relief washed over Cole. He'd rather trudge through a snake pit blindfolded, than to sit for thirty minutes at the same table with this insufferable woman. Although he was beside himself with exhilaration Jenna came back into his life, he imagined God was punishing him by sending Barbara Cassidy back into the picture too. What could he have ever done to justify such a painful castigation from the big guy? It was a thousand wonders how the motor-mouth got anywhere in life with the attitude of a psychopath.

After their food order had been taken, Cole noticed Jenna relaxing more. She leaned back in her chair and said, "I was so excited when I found out Cole had a brother. So, tell us a little about yourself."

"I'm afraid there's not much to tell," he responded, appearing uncomfortable with being thrown into the spotlight. "Honestly, I've been a drifter most of my life. My childhood was...let's just say different than most. I think it contributed to my rocky start in life."

"Yeah, I remember you telling me about Mom kicking you out of the house when you were fifteen, is that right?" Cole put in.

Dunston nodded. "I ended up bouncing around from one friend's house to another until I turned seventeen. From there I was on my own, doing what I could to survive on the streets. But when I turned twenty-six, I got lucky enough to meet a middle-aged man who was a damn good car mechanic. He took me under his wing and taught me how to fix cars. Since then, I've done enough of that to get by."

"That had to be tough," Barbara remarked. "I couldn't imagine being tossed out on your own at the age of fifteen."

"You know what they say," Dunston replied, "What doesn't kill you makes you stronger."

"Exactly, bro," Cole agreed. "It's that kind of mindset that got you through the hard times." Although he had been lucky enough to still have the woman who raised him to fall back on when the man believed to be his father was found dead, and thought to have been a notorious serial killer, the incident was devastating enough to destroy him if he would have let it. But that stubborn Rainwater determination to pick up the pieces and glue things back together again pulled him through, just as it did for Dunston. "So, out of curiosity, did you ever hear from Mom again?"

"Nope. As far as I was concerned, she was dead to me. All those years of living on the streets, forced to fend for myself, eating out of dumpsters, and sleeping where I could, has a way of hardening a man. I swore I'd never forgive her. Not after what I'd been forced to live through."

"God, Dunston," Jenna put in, "I'm so sorry that happened to you."

"Thank you, Jenna," Dunston replied. "But I survived it, and I do my best not to dwell on that low part of my life." He took a sip of water, and grinned as he set the glass down. "So, my brother here tells me you two are getting married."

Jenna's face beamed, and a smile bubbled up from inside Cole to see her perk up at the mention of their upcoming wedding. "We are," she said. "In less than a month if you can believe it."

"Well, congratulations." Dunston appeared genuinely happy for them. "That is news worth celebrating."

"About that," Cole said, "I wanted to ask if you'd be my best man."

Dunston's expression opened in surprise. "Are you serious, man? I mean, I wouldn't want to take the place of another good friend who has earned that position."

"I was going to ask a co-worker," Cole admitted. "The only good friend that comes to mind lives in Fort Worth. He's so far away, and is kept so busy running his ranch, I really didn't want to create a huge burden for him, ya know. You're my brother, and even though we just discovered each other, I'd really like you to stand beside me on the most important day of my life."

Cole was rewarded by a loving squeeze from Jenna. He stared at her and was deeply touched by the warmth in her eyes. "I think that would be perfect, Cole," she told him.

He turned to Dunston. "So, what do you say?"

Dunston smiled big. "I'd be honored, man."

"This is going to be the event of the year," Barb added, excitement in her voice.

Their food arrived, and after the server placed each meal in front of them, she set out four long-stemmed glasses, and poured wine into each one. Then she put an ice bucket in the middle of the table, slipping the bottle inside.

Jenna peered at Cole, surprise on her face. "Did you order a bottle of wine?"

Before Cole could respond, Dunston spoke up. "I ordered it when I arrived and told them to bring it out with our meal. I figured the news of the wedding deserved some celebrating."

"You didn't have to do that," Jenna said, even though the expression in her eyes said she was moved that he did.

Dunston raised his glass for a toast. "To Jenna and Cole. And to a lifetime of happiness together."

"Hear, hear," Barb added, raising her glass.

Four glasses clinked together.

After taking a sip, Cole set his on the table and said, "I have some more news worth celebrating." He faced his brother. "During the meeting with the trust attorney, I learned Hershel was a sixty percent shareholder in a company called Toys Galore. He passed those shares on to me, and I made a decision to sell them."

Barbara's mouth dropped open. "Are you kidding me? Jesus, Cole. That company has to be worth millions."

"My shares are worth a hundred-million to be precise."

That response threw Barb for a loop. "Holy shit. Why would you sell out with the amount of money you stand to make?"

"Because I didn't feel it was fair Hershel left those shares to me and did not split them between me and Dunston. So, I sold the shares and would like to give my brother half the money."

"Oh my God," Dunston said, shock ruling his expression. He appeared to be letting Cole's words sink in, and after shaking his head he answered, "It's a generous offer, but it's one I can't accept. If Hershel wanted me to have those shares, he would have turned them over to me. But he didn't. And the last thing I want is to become a charity case for anybody. I was forced to spend years living on the streets and taking handouts to survive. I haven't had to do that in years. I'm not that kid anymore. I believe in hard work, and I believe in earning my way through life."

That hadn't gone down the way Cole imagined. His brother appeared on the verge of being offended. "Listen, I didn't mean to insult your integrity. That's not at all why I made this decision. Hershel was a selfish man. He acquired his millions by extortion based on the pain of our grandmother. In my opinion, he didn't deserve his wealth, and he damn sure didn't earn it. Me and you, we didn't lie and cheat our way through life. We went through Hell while our great-grandfather sat back in luxury and didn't lift a finger to intervene, knowing he could have at any time. Justice was not served the way Hershel doled out the inheritance. But I can change that. I can ensure the right thing is done here. If I deserve those shares, so do you, Dunston. Just because Hershel didn't do the just thing, doesn't mean I should follow in his footsteps. What kind of man would I be if I did that?"

His brother peered down at the table. His body language told Cole he hadn't considered he'd felt that way. "I appreciate that, bro. Nothing humbles a person more than living on the streets and begging for meals. It made me grateful for the little things, and it showed me how to survive on very little. I'm not accustomed to taking more than I need. This whole inheritance thing," he said, putting his hands out, "is way more than I can deal with. I don't want you to make a rash decision based on what you think I need. I can survive on practically nothing."

"I can see that," Cole offered. "For what you've been through, you have the strength of an ox to have pulled through it. But this isn't about what I think you need. It's about doing the right thing. The thing I feel Hershel should have done."

Dunston's mouth lifted into a grin. "I get it, bro. And I can't say I wouldn't have done the same thing. Give me a little time to think about it. I still haven't recovered from the shock of all of this."

Cole frowned, lifting the bottle of wine out of the bucket and topping off all their glasses. "Fair enough, man. "Let's drink to thinking about it, then."

At the end of the evening, as Cole, Jenna, and Barbara headed toward the car in the parking lot of Hank's Steakhouse, he wondered why, with things going so smoothly, a sinking feeling the weight of a brick had settled in his gut. It made no sense. He was experiencing the best time of his life, with the new inheritance opening him up to more opportunities than he could have ever imagined. Discovering a brother he never knew he had, and most importantly, his soon to be marriage to the woman he loved with every beat of his heart. He should be on top of the world. But something threatening gnawed at his insides, a premonition that dark fate waited just around the corner.

He shook it off as he stepped to the passenger's side and opened the door for Jenna. But even as she settled in, the troubling sensation refused to go away. He shut her in and trudged over to his side of the vehicle. As he swept open the door, the excited chatter of Barbara and his fiancée filled the cab of the car.

Something Jenna said last night echoed in his mind. *If anything good happened to me, I always had to question it.* Is that what this was? Was his mind subconsciously thwarting the happiness he was experiencing because it seemed too good to be true? It certainly seemed logical. After all, the good luck he found himself having lately wasn't a usual occurrence, nor expected by any stretch of the imagination. *Stop being so damn critical.* Good things happen to good people. He wholeheartedly believed that. Or did he?

****

Cole met up with Jenna after work, and they both headed out to The Blazing Saddle Ranch in his truck. They'd been so busy up until now, there had been no time to check out the place he'd inherited from Hershel.

Once they drove to the outskirts of Dallas and approached the address on the GPS, the only indication they'd arrived was the house number and street stamped on a huge mailbox sitting a few feet off the road. Cole drove onto the pebble driveway and rolled past the line of manicured bushes placed attractively on both sides. When the mansion surfaced, it took his breath.

"Oh my God, Cole," Jenna whispered, gazing out the windshield in awe. "This is amazing."

It resembled a medieval castle, only with a modern flair. It stood three stories high, built with gray brick, giving it an ancient appearance. Cole was lost for words as he parked the truck and he and Jenna stepped out. He was so small, standing there, peering up at the enormous dwelling. It was obvious his great-grandfather spared no expense building this place. He found it unbelievable he now owned it.

Jenna ambled around to his side, and they joined

hands, heading toward the insanely large structure. As they approached a set of double doors big enough to drive a truck through, Cole no sooner took the key from his pocket, than the doors opened.

A tall woman with a blonde French braid appeared inside the doorway. Dressed in pressed, white shirt and black slacks. She smiled warmly while he read the words embroidered across the front of her blouse. The Blazing Saddle Ranch. "Welcome to your new home, Mr. Rainwater and Ms. Langley," the woman said in an unusually deep voice.

Cole stared at her, as if doing so would explain who this woman was and how she knew who they were.

"Pardon me," she said. "I can see your confusion. I'm Cecilia Dowers, the manager here at the ranch. I'm one of ten staff members on board. It's my duty to oversee daily operations."

"Daily operations?" He was more confused by her explanation.

"We have a chef, as well as a few ranch hands, a butler, and house maids."

"You're kidding me," Jenna said, stunned.

"No, ma'am. Without us to tend to the needs of the grounds and the mansion, I'm afraid The Blazing Saddle Ranch would fall into disrepair."

"How long have you worked here?" Cole wanted to know. In his letter, Hershel did not mention the fully employed staff, that no doubt, he would now be responsible to pay.

"Mr. Rainwater hired us when he built this place fifteen years ago. But he didn't want you to worry when you took over ownership of the ranch. He has paid our salary for the next five years."

There was a new surprise waiting for him every day where it concerned his great-grandfather and his estates and business dealings. But the man certainly put necessary steps in place for a smooth transition.

"We have been awaiting your arrival, Mr. Rainwater," an older, handsome man said coming to a stop beside Cecilia. "My name is Clemens Rhodes, and I'm the butler here at The Blazing Saddle Ranch. I want to assure you the utmost care has been taken to prepare for your visit."

Cole scratched his head. "And how did you know when I would visit?"

"We didn't, sir. But we have been preparing since the day Jim Carter informed us he spoke with you about your great-grandfather's trust."

Cole remembered Jim Carter as being the trust attorney he and Dunston met with a few days ago.

"If you'll follow me, sir," Clemens said, "I'll show you and Ms. Langley to the trophy room while I gather the staff to meet you."

"The trophy room?" Jenna whispered as they let the butler lead them into the house.

Cole was taken in by the incredible sight of the wooden carvings winding up the largest mahogany staircase he'd ever seen. Then Clemens' voice echoed back to them, stealing away his attention. "To better clarify, Ms. Langley, it's called the trophy room because of the amount of exotic game mounted on the walls. Hershel was quite the hunter."

When Cole glanced back at Jenna, coming up beside him, her reaction to the butler's words was a disapproving scowl. No doubt, the display of stuffed creatures would be the first thing to go.

And once they entered the room, his earlier conviction intensified. If it weren't for the furniture placed throughout, and the fireplace against the farthest wall, he'd swear he just stepped into a jungle.

Clemens pointed toward one of the huge sofas. If you'll have a seat, I will go and fetch the staff."

The man no sooner stepped from the room when Jenna grimaced. "This is hideous. These poor animals. Who could be so cruel?"

Cole grinned, shrinking down into the sofa beside her. "It's most likely not what you think. You remember Dario, right?"

She nodded. "That's the guy who owned the horse ranch you took me and Emily horseback riding on."

"Occasionally, he used to go on these trophy hunts in Africa. Many of the villages out there are threatened by an overpopulation of these kinds of animals. They kill off livestock, wreak havoc on plowing fields, and in some cases, kill off the villagers. So, the villagers will sometimes allow hunters from all over the world to come in and hunt the animals that are destroying their livelihoods. And the hunters pay well for the opportunity to hunt these animals. The villagers often use that money for things such as installing toilets and waterpipes and building houses for the poorest among them."

Even though he could tell she had a better understanding of why trophy hunting took place, she was in no way convinced to keep Hershel's collection. "I just don't want them in the house. I can't help but feel badly for them."

"Then they're gone. Simple as that."

"Thank you."

When Clemens marched back into the room, there were many new faces following in his wake. The staff lined up in perfect order a few feet in front of Cole and Jenna. Clemens started from the right side of the line, introducing each member with a description of their duties.

It was the strangest thing Cole ever experienced. When had there ever been this many people at the ready to serve him? Never, that's when. It was an uncomfortable feeling, and it struck him whether there would ever be any getting used to this kind of treatment. But he had become a wealthy man overnight. Life would never be the same.

"Sara can take you and Ms. Langley on a tour of the house, Mr. Rainwater," Clemens announced.

The young woman in question tipped her head, and stepped forward in perfect form, as if she were a soldier being called to the front of the line by her sergeant.

"Then we will have the jeep ready to take you on a tour of the ranch," Clemens added.

Sara smiled gracefully and said, "Mr. Rainwater. Ms. Langley. Whenever you're ready."

During the exploration of the mansion, Cole found it amazing how well Sara took to Jenna. Before they'd approached the third room, his fiancée managed to break the young lady out of her shell, and the two were chatting up a storm. It was no shock she knew how to handle people and situations better than him. She'd had the talent since they were teenagers. It had been one of the things he loved most about her.

Although Cole was completely taken in by the timeless beauty of the mansion he'd inherited, his interest lay in the two-hundred acres outside the dwelling. And as he'd hoped, the tour of the grounds did not disappoint. There were two massive horse stables in all, and a large riding arena. Upon seeing it, a feeling of euphoria settled in his chest. Emily would fall in love with it. She'd be out here so often sharpening her riding skills, it would most likely be a challenge to get her to come indoors. But it would be perfect because he'd be right here with her doing what he loved the most, riding.

When Cole settled his eyes on Blaze, Hershel's prized stallion, he had no doubt why the man named his ranch after the animal. He was exceptionally tall, with a raven, shiny coat that would have been the envy of many prestigious show horses. An image of him perched on the back of this proud boy, riding like thunder through the meadows, made Cole dreamy-eyed. A wave of excitement rippled through him. He could hardly wait to saddle him up and get out into the open. But that would have to wait. The other seven horses were good, strong breeds, and appeared to be just as well-groomed and cared for.

By the time they reentered the mansion, Jenna was smiling from ear to ear, and adrenaline pumped through him, causing a high he was sure would last for days. This would be the perfect place for them. He felt it down to his soul.

As if in sync with his thoughts, Jenna said, "It's wonderful, Cole! When do we get to move in?"

He laughed, sidling up beside her and taking her hand. "We can move in whenever you want, sweetheart."

"Great. Then tomorrow, I'll call and schedule an

appointment with the movers."

"That won't be necessary, Ms. Langley." Cecilia's deep voice floated into the foyer as she entered the room and approached them. "We'll take care of everything for you." She handed Jenna a business card, saying, "My direct cell phone number is on there. All you need to do is call and let me know what day you'd like us to get everything moved for you."

This was the second time the staff seemed to hear them when they should have been out of earshot. First when Jenna whispered to him about the trophy room and Clemens answered, and just now. Cole had been sure no one was in the room to know what Jenna said. Did the place have ears? That creeped him out, and he spoke up. "Pardon my bluntness. But you guys aren't listening in on us, are you?"

At first Cecilia appeared speechless. And then she smiled with understanding. "It's not meant to make you uncomfortable, Mr. Rainwater. But your great-grandfather had listening devices placed in every room. Of course, except for the master suite, upstairs. All of the staff wear earpieces," she admitted, lifting the hair away from her left ear to expose the small, white receiver.

"Why would he do that?"

"Because he wanted to make sure we knew the moment he needed us."

Cole was blown away by this knowledge. "So, he wanted you at his beck and call?"

She frowned. "For lack of a better word, yes. That's what the devices are for."

"Cecilia," Jenna said, "We won't need the staff to do that. Please have someone remove the listening devices. We'd much rather have our privacy. And we won't need you guys running after our every need. Me and Cole can handle a lot ourselves."

The woman appeared confused. "But the mansion is so big, if you needed us, how will we know?"

"Why don't we work out a schedule?" Jenna suggested. "We'll have a set time for dinner and other daily activities. If we need anything in between that we can't manage on our own, we have your number, and we'll call you."

"Of course, Ms. Langley. If that's the way you wish it."

"And please, call me Jenna. And I'll call you Cecilia. Okay?"

The woman nodded, although the expression on her face made it obvious she wasn't quite sure how to take them.

"We're very down to earth," Cole explained. "To be honest, we're not used to all this. We're just an average, middle-class family who happened to come into a wealthy inheritance. I hope you understand what I'm getting at."

"I understand, Mr. Rainwater."

It was apparent she didn't. Cole wanted to, like Jenna, ask her to call him by his first name.

Something told him it would be a challenge for her to remember to do that and would probably result in her feeling badly when she'd forgotten. This was going to take some time but removing the listening devices would be a start. "And if you don't mind, Cecilia," he said as an afterthought, "would you mind getting rid of the animals in the trophy room? Jenna is uncomfortable with them here."

"I'll have Clemens start working on that today."

He nodded. "Thank you."

Jenna's phone rang. She slipped it out of her pocket, and after examining the number, turned to Cole. "It's Ava."

She strolled off to get some privacy, he imagined, from the all-hearing ears of Cecilia. The idea of his fiancée working with an ex-girlfriend to plan their wedding still hadn't sunk in. He'd left the decision up to Jenna, asserting a level of acceptance with whatever she wanted to do. But convincing himself it would all work out was not as concrete an idea as it should have been. It wasn't the lack of trust in her judgement, or the unpredictability of Ava's future behavior that bothered him, since the only time he'd witnessed the woman act out of sorts had been that day in the restaurant, and there were serious doubts she'd do it again. The whole thing carried a sensation of something close to taboo. Since that phone conversation with Jenna, a foreboding sensation had developed. And it was something he hadn't been able to shake since.

Jenna sashayed back with the phone cradled in her hand. "Ava wants to know what time you and Dunston can meet her at the tailor's tomorrow for a fitting."

"I'll probably get off work at six. I don't think Dunston has any plans tomorrow. If you're getting off work at the same time, we can all go together."

She put the phone against her ear and relayed the information. After a brief pause, she pressed the device to her chest. "Six won't work. She's saying the tailor's office closes at four-thirty."

He frowned. "We'll just have to make it earlier then. What's the latest we can arrive?"

After asking, Jenna reported, "The tailor will probably need an hour between the two of you."

"So, three-thirty?"

"That should work."

"I can fit that in, and I'm sure Dunston can as well. What about you?"

With an expression of hesitancy, Jenna said, "I have a meeting at three o'clock with a business owner. We have a lot to go over, and I don't think we'll wrap things up in time. I really need that account."

"So, me and Dunston will need to go without you?"

It wasn't the ideal thing to do. For whatever reason, being alone with Ava was an uncomfortable concept. It had been why he'd suggested Jenna go with him and Dunston to begin with. Then again, he wouldn't be alone with Ava. Dunston would be there, too.

"If you're okay with that?" she said, carefully monitoring his expression.

Cole shrugged off his uncertainty. "That'll be fine."

"Great. Then that'll give me enough time to finish with my meeting, and I'd be able to meet you at the venue Ava wants to show us for the reception." She got back on the phone with Ava before Cole could say another word.

Like it or not. That's the way it was going to be.

Chapter Six

Cole and Dunston stood outside the tailor's shop waiting for Ava to arrive. Three-thirty had already come and gone; he was starting to consider the idea of rescheduling. Just as he slid his phone out of his pocket to check the time again, it rang in his hand. A strange number popped up.

"Hello," he said, staring at his brother who stood a few feet in front of him, his long frame leaning against the hood of his clunker with legs crossed in a negligent posture.

"Cole?" a female voice said.

"This is him."

"Hi, it's Ava."

Uncomfortable, he shifted the phone to his other ear. "How did you get my number?"

"Oh, sorry. I called Jenna to get it. I'm running a bit behind, and I didn't want you to wonder where I was."

He didn't respond. It sure as hell wasn't kosher that she now had his phone number.

"Are you there, Cole?"

He sighed, shaking his head, not the least bit happy with the situation. "Where are you?"

"About five minutes away. Did you go in yet?"

"I wasn't sure what you needed us to do."

"I've called David the store owner; he's expecting

you guys. You can go in. He's already got some tuxedos picked out for you and Dunston to try on. I'll be there as soon as I can."

"All right." He ended the call, eyeing Dunston's ancient car. "When in the hell are you going to trade that piece of shit in for a real car? No offense, bro. But you now have serious dough to upgrade."

Dunston gave the heap a look and laughed. "You got a point."

"Damn right I do. Go get one of those classy muscle cars. Hell, go get something that has a full coat of paint. Something with a bumper that doesn't look like you stole it from a junkyard."

"Hey, now," his brother warned. "Betsy's got me where I needed to go for years."

"Yeah, well, Betsy's tired, man. Just look at her."

They both busted out in laughter as Cole slipped the phone into the inside pocket of his suit jacket. Getting back to the subject, he said, "That was the wedding planner. She's late—no duh—and we should head inside. Evidently, they have tuxedos ready for us to try on."

Both men headed into the office, and a short, balding man stood by the door waiting for them. "Mr. Rainwater, I'm David. I just heard from Ava. She's been delayed."

"I know," he answered. "I just got off the phone with her."

"Not to worry. We've got you all fixed up. If you gentlemen will go see Cindy," he said, gesturing toward the back of the shop. "She'll show you to the dressing rooms."

An attractive redhead approached from the back

with garments hanging over her arm. "Here are your tuxedos," she said, handing them out. "Go ahead to the back, just beyond those racks." She pointed toward the rear of the shop, "You'll see the dressing rooms. Holler for me if you need anything, okay?"

As they headed in that direction, she called out to Cole, "You can leave your suit jacket on the bench outside of the dressing room. I'll take care of it for you. We wouldn't want it to wrinkle."

After doing her bidding, he stepped into the dressing room, closing the curtain behind him, and slid out of his shoes. As he changed, he wanted to get this over with, and slipped into the tuxedo as quickly as he could manage. Picking out clothes for a wedding, even if it was for his own, wasn't exactly a man's thing. And although he hadn't seen Ava since the restaurant, there existed no doubt dealing with her would get on his nerves. When Jenna had made the decision to hire her as their wedding planner, he figured she'd be spending more time with the woman than he would. But here he was without his fiancée and left to handle things with Ava on his own. There'd be no fun in that.

Stepping out of the dressing cubicle, his attention glazed over Dunston standing there waiting for him and wondered how he managed to get changed so quickly. The tuxedo his brother wore was similar to his, only with a silky, blue bowtie, instead of a red one like his.

"Oh, just look at you," Ava said, coming toward him with a satisfied grin. "Don't you look handsome."

"Thank you," he said, intentionally striding straight past her to stand in front of the mirror.

As he stood there, he noticed her reflection coming up behind him. She laid a hand on his shoulder. "How does it feel?"

For a split second he caught an expression in her eyes that made it seem as if she wasn't talking about the tuxedo. Uncomfortable, he took two steps to one side. "Fine. I think this will work."

Cindy joined them. "You look stunning, dear. I think this is a perfect fit for you."

The shop helper stepped in front of him and fiddled with his bowtie. "There," she said, flattening out the shoulders, and running her hands down the arms of the garment. "Perfect. You are very handsome in that tuxedo, Mr. Rainwater."

Before he could thank her for her kind words, her attention turned to Dunston who was approaching. "Let's see if another pair of slacks will work for you," she told his brother, ambling past him and heading toward a clothing rack. "I think those are a bit too long."

"I never congratulated you on your upcoming marriage," Ava said to Cole, as he turned back toward the mirror. "Jenna is a wonderful person, and I couldn't be happier for you two."

As he stared at her reflection, he had to admit she seemed sincere. Perhaps, he had been too hard on her, and Jenna was right concerning her intuition about Ava. Maybe she did want to make amends for her unacceptable behavior at the restaurant. Was it possible he'd misread her intentions when she'd touched his shoulder a few minutes ago?

He lowered his head as a stab of guilt sliced through him for his eagerness to jump to conclusions. "Thank you," he said, peering back in the mirror at her reflection. "That means a lot to me. And you're right.

Jenna is amazing. I'm lucky to have her back in my life."

After finishing up with the fitting, Cole walked with Dunston out to his car. "I've decided to make the move to Arlington," his brother announced. "I've got to get my stuff brought over from Amarillo, but…"

Cole smiled and clapped him on the back. "Man, that's great. I'm glad to hear that. We'll be a whole lot closer to one another."

"Yeah, that's a big part of why I'm doing this."

"That's cool, bro." As Dunston swung open the car door, Cole said, "I've gotta' go over here and check out this venue for the wedding reception. You wanna' come along?"

Dunston shook his head, climbing into the car. "Can't," he said, staring at him with a lopsided grin. "I have a dinner date with Barbara. I need to head back to the inn and get showered up."

Cole pursed his lips. "A date with Barb, huh? Really?"

"What's wrong with that?"

Cole shrugged. "Nothing. She's not my type or wouldn't be for anyone with a brain, but…'

Dunston grinned as he slipped the key into the ignition and fired up the engine. "I think she's right about you. You *are* an asshole."

Cole laughed. "I have to hand it to her. She's probably right on the money about that." He let go of his brother's car door and backed away. "Okay, well, I'll see you later then."

Dunston waved a hand and shut himself inside the car.

As Cole made his way across the parking lot to his

truck, he noticed Ava reversing out of her parking space. He climbed into his vehicle and started it up. The radio blinked to life, and according to the clock, he ought to make it to the venue at about the same time Jenna did. He couldn't wait to see her.

****

Jenna glanced at the time on her phone as she headed out across the parking lot of her office. Damn, it took forever to wrap things up with the new client. Gazing at the clock on the wall and dropping signals to end the conversation as the man had rambled on incessantly had done nothing to help goad him out of the door any quicker. Now she was running at least ten minutes late.

She clicked the key fob to unlock the car as she approached it, swung open the door, and tossed her satchel into the passenger's seat. Peering out the windshield, she slipped the key in the ignition, noticing traffic on the highway in front of the office appeared light. Good. If luck held out, shaving a few minutes off the drive due to smooth, flowing traffic shouldn't be a problem.

She turned over the ignition. The engine sputtered and stalled. That was strange. Jenna twisted the key again, and this time nothing happened. Great.

Popping the hood and getting out to inspect the battery didn't solve the mystery. The damn thing appeared fine. There was no rust or build-up of any kind around the terminals. She hadn't owned the car for very long and had purchased it brand new without Cole's help. This vehicle was her pride and joy. Being able to purchase it on her own was proof that moving from Georgia to Texas after selling her janitorial company and opening a business consulting firm had been a smart decision, and a lucrative one at that. Now she frowned at the mechanical dilemma she faced. If it wasn't the battery, then what was it?

The sun beat down on the parking lot, causing the shiny, metal parts under the hood to flash brightly as if they were under a magnifying glass. She turned away as sweat dripped from her forehead and temples, getting into her eyes. Damn the luck. She could stand out here all day in the sweltering heat and never figure out what the problem was. *Face it, you're no mechanic.*

Cursing, she marched back to the passenger side of the car and snatched her phone from the console. She dialed Cole's number. It rang several times. "C'mon. answer the phone."

When it went to voicemail, she tried again. Nothing. "Son-of-a-bitch!" she cried in frustration, kicking the blasted tire. *That should make the car start, you dumbass.* It would be best to calm down and think. After taking a deep breath, the realization sank in a mechanic would have to be called. It was hotter than Hades out here and standing around being pissed and sweaty wasn't fixing the problem.

Jenna dialed the first mechanic whose name popped up on the search bar of her phone, not giving a damn how much it cost. She needed help now.

A man answered, and she explained the situation, asking how quickly they could get to her. "Give me about fifteen minutes, ma'am. I'll send a wrecker now."

Thank God. Now, how to get word to Cole. Then it hit her. She must be an idiot. Why in hell didn't she think to call Ava? She and Cole were together.

Was that why he wasn't answering her phone

calls?

"Oh my God," she said, hardly believing the awful thought that popped into her mind.

What was wrong with her? Cole had never shown he was less than trustworthy. But Ava? The scene from the restaurant tumbled back with a vengeance. The jealous way the woman acted. How she fawned all over Cole while Jenna sat there.

You're being ridiculous. Cole would never allow advances from another woman...even if he used to sleep with her.

Anger reared its ugly head. She had to calm herself down by remembering she'd been the one who set this up to begin with. It had been her who made the decision to hire Ava, not Cole. It was because she had empathy for the woman. And because she wanted to prove to Cole she was woman enough to handle this situation, that she wasn't jealous, and she trusted him completely.

So, trust him already. Finally, with a cool head, she dialed Ava's number.

"Hello, Jenna?"

It sounded like she was driving. With a huge sigh of relief, she answered, "I'm stuck here at the office. My car won't start. Do you know where Cole is? He's not answering his phone."

"He should be on his way to the venue. That's where I'm headed now. Do you want me to turn around and get you? I'm probably about twenty-five minutes away."

As Jenna opened her mouth to suggest that might be a good idea since Cole wasn't answering her calls, the wrecker drove into the parking lot. She thought better of it. "The wrecker is here now. I should go with him to the mechanic shop to see what's wrong with my car. The second you see Cole can you please tell him to call me? I really need to get in touch with him as soon as possible."

"I sure will."

"Thank you. I gotta' go."

As she pointed the wrecker to her stalled car, regret for the suspicious way she'd reacted concerning Cole and Ava settled to the bottom of her heart. Truth be told, although she wanted to be the bigger person and forgive Ava, she was still a tinge jealous over the attention the woman showered on Cole that day.

But it was her personal conviction, and it was something she needed to put behind her. Obviously, there was nothing going on between the two of them. She didn't doubt for a minute her fiancé loved her more than any man in the world. He wouldn't allow anything to jeopardize that.

****

When Cole drove into the parking lot at The Vine of McKinney and got out of his vehicle, he found Ava waiting on the broad, front steps. She shielded her eyes from the sun as he sidled up. Although he hadn't spotted Jenna's car in the parking lot, he figured she should be along any minute.

As he took the fifth step, Ava met him, got within an inch of his face, and took his hand. Before he could react to the unexpected contact, she said, "I have something that belongs to you."

A cool object touched his palm, and he glanced down as she closed his fingers around it.

When he realized what it was, he peered up at her, took a step back to put some distance between them, and said, "How did you get my phone? I didn't even know It was missing."

A silly grin spread across her face when she said, "I grabbed it at the tailor's. I thought it was mine, and I didn't realize the mistake until I got here."

Cole frowned, instinctively shoving his hand into the pocket of his suit jacket, the last place he remembered putting the device. "I never took the phone out of my pocket."

"You must have. It was lying on the bench outside the dressing room. When I was over there, I think that's when I grabbed it assuming it was mine. But I'd left mine in my purse the whole time."

"Are you talking about the bench outside the dressing room I was in?"

"I think so."

"But I never saw you over there."

She appeared stunned, and said, "I was sitting on the bench waiting for you to get finished changing."

"No, you weren't, Ava. When I got out of the dressing cubicle, you weren't anywhere near the bench."

She furrowed her brows, expression twisting in irritation. "Of course, I was. How else would I get your phone?"

"I don't know," he snapped, more agitated than dumbfounded. "You weren't sitting on that bench, and I never took the phone out of my jacket pocket."

"Do you think I stole your phone? Why would I do that?"

Her words penetrated in his mind. Why would she purposely take his phone?

"Maybe the phone fell out of your jacket," she

offered.

He reflected on what occurred when he laid his jacket on the bench. Then he remembered Cindy telling him she would take care of it to keep it from wrinkling. Come to think of it, he didn't recall seeing the jacket on the bench when he stepped out of the cubicle. Before he left the establishment, Cindy handed him the jacket. It was plausible when she removed the jacket from the bench, his phone had slipped out. However, when he'd headed out of the dressing area after changing into the tuxedo, Ava was not on that bench waiting for him. Why was she insisting she was?

It didn't matter. Like before at the tailor's shop, he was ready to get this over with. Without Jenna, none of this had been a pleasant experience. And that brought him to his first concern. He turned, scanning the parking lot, but she was nowhere in sight.

He faced Ava. "Jenna should have been here already. Now that I have my phone, I'll give her a call and see what's taking her."

"Oh, I almost forgot. She called me on the way here. She was having car trouble. I offered to turn around and pick her up, but she wanted to go with the wrecker to the mechanic shop to see what was up with the car. She didn't think she was going to make it, so she wanted us to go ahead and check out the venue and call her when we're through."

Cole didn't like the sound of that. "Are you sure? Maybe I should call her."

Ava made a show of glancing at her watch. "We should have already gone in ten minutes ago. They have another couple that will be arriving here in about five more minutes to book this place for the same day you and Jenna wanted it for. The manager assured me he would let us have it if we got here first. So, we really need to get inside now. This shouldn't take long. We just need to take a quick peek around, and get the paperwork signed. This is the perfect place for the reception. And I'm afraid if we don't get this booked, we may not find anything else available for the time slot you guys wanted."

Cole sighed and shook his head. "All right. But let's make this quick. I really need to get in touch with Jenna."

"I promise. Just give me ten minutes at the most."

"Let's go."

No matter what, he wouldn't let her take a minute longer.

****

Jenna plopped down on the worn, cracked, leather chair inside the waiting area of the mechanic shop. The air-conditioner was a window unit with greasy fingerprints covering damn near every inch of it. The thing hummed and buzzed loudly, rattling the window frame that encased it. Despite the noise and grease, Jenna was grateful for the cool air pumping out. Wisps of hair once drenched in sweat had dried, now plastered to her face. Damp material clung to her flesh, giving off the sensation of being dipped in water and then stuffed inside a meat freezer.

The desire to be home and stepping into a heavenly shower right now was overwhelming. Maybe if she called Cole, he'd answer his phone, despite the fact he hadn't answered any of the calls she continued to make while riding to the mechanic shop with the guy who drove her here.

As she fished her phone out of her purse, it rang. Thank God, it must be Cole, finally.

It was Barbara instead. She answered, disappointed it wasn't who she wanted it to be. "Hey."

"What are you doing?"

"Sitting at the mechanic shop, waiting for them to fix my car."

"Oh, no. What happened?"

"I don't know. When I went to leave my office, it wouldn't start so I had to call a mechanic. They sent a wrecker to pick up my car."

"Where's Cole?"

"With Ava checking out a venue for the wedding reception."

"Wait a minute. I thought you told me you were going to that."

"I was supposed to. I couldn't make it to the fitting with Cole and Dunston. So, after the meeting with a new client, I was going to meet Ava and Cole at the venue. But my car wouldn't start."

"Cole knows, right? And he still went to the venue with Ava while you're stuck at the mechanic's shop?"

Jenna's attention floated toward the ceiling. She'd had a crappy enough day without her best friend giving her a hard time about something she knew nothing about. "He didn't leave me stuck at the mechanic shop, Barbara. He doesn't know my car broke down. I called Ava when I couldn't get in touch with him. She was headed to the venue and assured me she'd let him know I've been trying to get hold of him. I'm waiting on him to call me now."

"How long ago was that?"

Jenna drew the phone away long enough to glance

at the time. She didn't realize it, but twenty-five minutes had ticked by since she talked to Ava. She should have arrived at the venue by now and given Cole the message. Why hadn't he called her? "I don't know why he hasn't been answering his phone."

"I told you not to trust that woman."

"C'mon, Barb." Even as the words left her mouth, second thoughts about the wisdom of hiring one of Cole's ex-girlfriends to plan their wedding—especially one who acted so atrociously the first time they'd met—rose up and waved fat red flags in her face. "I trust Cole. Do you really think he'd cheat on me?"

"What's to stop Ava from trying to sabotage your wedding by trying to get back together with him?"

"Not gonna' happen. Besides, you saw her at the wedding planner's office. If that wasn't remorse, I don't know what is."

"You don't know her true intentions. You only see what she wants you to see."

Jenna wanted to hear this from Barbara about as much as she desired to be told she contracted a deadly disease and had one week to live. These haunting thoughts were already hounding her to the point of practically driving her insane. Her friend wasn't making it any easier. "Listen, I'm going to try to call Cole again. Hopefully, he answers his phone this time."

"Okay. Call me back if you can't get hold of him and you need a ride home. I have a date with Dunston tonight, but he'll just have to wait if you need me to come get you."

"A hot date with Dunston, huh?"

"Don't sound so surprised. You know I like him."

"He is kinda cute, isn't he?"

"Honey, he's hot. I plan on getting to know him really well if that's any indication."

Jenna laughed, her spirits lifting a bit. "Have fun tonight."

"Call me if you need me, Jenna. I'm dead serious."

Even though Barb had a sure way of getting on her nerves often. She had no doubt her best friend would drop everything to be there for her in a heartbeat. "I will. But I'm going to get in touch with Cole. Let me get off the phone so I can call him."

"All right. I'll keep my phone close by. Let me know if you get hold of him."

"I will. Bye."

"Ms. Langley."

Jenna peered up to find a lanky mechanic standing by the door. "Yes."

"We're going to need more time with your car."

"How long?"

"Not sure. It seems like an exhaust problem. We'll know more tomorrow."

She frowned, wondering how a car as new as this one could be having those kinds of problems so soon. "Okay. Thank you. I'll call my fiancé to have him pick me up."

"No problem, ma'am. Take your time."

****

With the documents for the venue rental having been signed, Cole marched through the doors and down the steps, grabbing for his phone to call Jenna, find out the location of the mechanic shop, and let her know not to worry, that he was on his way.

He stopped briefly to search his contacts for her number, when he noticed several missed calls from her.

Damn, she'd tried to get in touch with him repeatedly when Ava had his phone. But before he had the chance to hit dial, someone grabbed his arm, startling him.

"So, what did you think?" Ava said, settling in beside him.

His mind drew a blank.

"About the venue, silly. Isn't it the perfect place for the wedding reception?"

"Yeah, it's great." It wasn't as if he'd paid much attention to the details of the tour. He just wanted to get through the blasted excursion as quickly as possible so he could call Jenna.

The moment his attention focused back on the device, Ava said, "Wait, Cole?"

He no sooner glanced up, then the woman's lips crashed down on his.

Confusion swirled around his mind, thoughts running in a thousand different directions. The second he regained his senses, he wrenched away. Anger boiled like a pressure cooker deep inside, threatening to explode. "What the hell do you think you're doing?"

She glared at him with a stunned expression. Her lips trembled. Eyes twitched. "I—I, uh—"

The phone in his hand rang. Jenna's number popped up on the screen, and his heartrate picked up. An instant sweat washed over him. It jingled again, and Cole took a step back, catching himself before tripping down the step he hadn't realized was directly behind him. He turned to face the parking lot and plodded down the concrete stairs, swiping his finger across the phone and putting it against his ear. "Jenna?"

"Oh my God!" Her tone was filled with exasperation. "I thought I'd never get a hold of you.

Why weren't you answering my calls?"

"I'm so sorry, honey," he said, rushing across the parking lot to his truck. Every inch he put between him and the woman who had just kissed him felt like a mile. "Ava accidentally grabbed my phone at the tailor's shop thinking it was hers."

"I called her. Why didn't she tell me that?"

"I don't think she realized it until she got to the venue."

"Oh. Did she give you my message?"

"Yes. And I wanted to call you right away, but by the time we arrived, there was another couple on their way here to book the same day we wanted. I had to rush to get the paperwork signed before that happened."

After approaching the truck and opening the door, he caught sight of Ava out of the corner of his eye. She was headed straight for him. Turning to face her, he put out a hand, staving off her advances. She stopped and just stood there, anxiety pinching the corners of her face.

Jenna said, "Did you book it?"

Cole spun on his heels, resting his arm over the frame of the door for support. He took a deep breath, attempting to rein in the adrenaline pumping through him like a lightning bolt. "It's reserved. In fact, I literally just walked out of there."

"I'm glad at least that went well."

If she only knew what Ava did to him. "What's wrong with your car?"

She sighed heavily. "The mechanics don't exactly know yet. They need to keep it overnight. One of them said something about a possible exhaust problem."

That didn't sound right. The damn thing was only a

few months old. "Are you sure that's what he said?"

"Yeah. They'll know more tomorrow."

"Okay. Text me the address, babe, and I'll be on my way to get you."

"Thank God. You wouldn't believe how sweaty I am. I just want to go home and take a shower."

A pang of guilt stabbed at his heart for what she must have been going through while he had been caught up in his own little world and becoming victim to Ava's dirty tricks. If he would have known the lunatic was going to force herself on him, he would have told the bitch to shove this whole thing up her ass.

"When we get home, I will start you a shower and fix you a meal. I imagine you have to be starved."

A pause and then, "I love you, Cole."

Those words were like a slingshot, hitting him where it hurt. "I love you too, sweetheart. Don't forget to text me the address."

"I will. Just please hurry."

As soon as it was apparent the call had ended, Ava continued toward him.

He hurriedly climbed into the truck. "Go away, Ava. I don't want to hear anything you have to say."

"Jesus, I'm sorry, Cole," she confessed, slowing her steps as she approached the vehicle. "I can't believe I did that."

"Yeah, neither can I," he replied, shaking his head in disgust, and thrusting his hand into his pocket for the keys.

"Wait, give me a chance to apologize."

He smirked putting the key into the ignition. "You already did."

As he put his hand out for the door, she grabbed it.

"I meant explain. Please let me explain."

"I don't have time. Jenna is waiting for me. Now, let go of the door."

"Are you going to tell her?"

He lowered his head, knowing he had a duty to do just that. "Yeah. I probably will. Me and Jenna don't keep secrets from each other."

He had no idea how he planned to inform his fiancée his ex-girlfriend kissed him on the front steps of the venue he had rented for their wedding reception. Jenna was already stressed enough. He couldn't imagine how being forced to find another wedding planner so close to the wedding was going to affect her.

"Please don't," Ava pleaded. "It will only make it worse."

It probably would. But he didn't know if he could live with being dishonest with her. "Why did you kiss me?"

The woman stared at the ground, her body language telling him she didn't have a good answer. "I don't know...the way things ended between us when you broke it off with me. I guess I never recovered from it. I really cared for you. And then you were out of my life just like that."

"Look, Ava—"

"I know. You were in love with Jenna. You couldn't commit to me because of it. I understand. But it doesn't make it hurt any less."

Cole sighed and peered down. Although, in a way he felt badly for the way he broke things off with Ava, in his heart he knew it was better to have done that than allowed her to continue living a lie. It would never have worked out, and she had to have seen that. "My intention was never to hurt you. In the end, I felt leading you on would have hurt you more."

"You're right. It would have."

"If you still felt this way, why did you convince Jenna to hire you to plan our wedding?" He couldn't wrap his head around that.

"Wishful thinking, I guess. I'd convinced myself I'd gotten over you. And to be honest, I really did feel terrible about treating Jenna so rudely. I wanted to make it up to her, and I thought if I made her wedding special, she would forgive me, and I could forgive myself."

"So, you thought seducing her fiancé would make her wedding extra special?"

"I didn't plan to do that. It just happened."

"I hope you see now how this isn't going to work."

She glanced away and took a deep breath. When her eyes met his again, there was an expression of determination in them. "I think it still can."

Cole shook his head, not believing what just came out of her mouth. "You just kissed me."

"I know. And I swear to God it will never happen again."

"You're damn right it won't because we're finding another wedding planner."

"Okay. I understand. But I'm begging you not to tell Jenna what happened. She's so stressed right now. I can see it in her eyes. She'll be the one who suffers the most out of this."

He turned the key in the ignition and said, tightly, "Let go of the door. Jenna is exhausted, and she's waiting for me."

After a moment, she let go and backed away. "I'm

just asking you to think about it, all right? I don't see a reason to hurt Jenna."

After Ava cleared the parking lot, he checked Jenna's text for the address, punched it into the GPS, shut the door, threw the gearshift in reverse, and then pointed the truck toward the highway, completely beside himself. As much as he hated to admit it, she was right. Jenna would be the one hurt the most out of all of them. Yet he had a responsibility to tell her the truth. If he kept this from her and she found out, he didn't know how easily she could forgive him, not to mention the damage such a thing would do to their relationship.

But then, how would she find out? Ava certainly wasn't going to tell her. But if he didn't tell her, how could he justify the need to find another wedding planner? He sure as hell wasn't going near Ava ever again. His brain hurt from all the scenarios running through his mind. He found himself agonizingly torn between hurting Jenna with the truth and protecting her with a lie. Perhaps Ava was right, and everything can carry on as normal. That was the most asinine idea that ever entered his head. Of course, things could never go back to what they were before that damned kiss wrecked everything. The situation had been at least bearable before Ava came along and blew that out of the water. Now what? He had to tell her.

Or keep it to himself and spare her the hurt.

The turn for Bloomingdale Road was approaching. A decision would have to be reached before Jenna climbed into the truck. What's it going to be?

She shouldn't have to suffer because of Ava's impulsiveness. He could forget the kiss. It meant nothing. The alternative would bring about more stress for Jenna, and additional bad dreams. She was just beginning to feel better, and to get a grip on things. Could he convince her to hire another wedding planner without telling her what happened? No. She would question his motive for that suggestion. What reasonable excuse could he come up with? And wasn't it defeating the purpose of not telling her if he wasn't going to spare her the stress of finding another wedding planner so close to the wedding? He didn't know if he could bear to look at Ava, let alone pretend everything was fine for the next few weeks. But his discomfort wasn't what was in question here. He'd manage to get through it. Jenna had been the main concern in all of this.

Okay, I'll tell her. After the wedding, and when this is all over, I'll sit her down and tell her what Ava did. And I'll explain why I didn't say anything earlier. She loved him, and she knew his heart. She would understand he didn't want to upset her. But right now, before the wedding, he couldn't risk the anxiety this would undoubtedly bring upon her. Until then, he'd keep his distance from Ava. Make sure they would never be alone again.

Jenna stepped out of the office the moment Cole drove up to the mechanic's shop. She appeared sweaty and exhausted, just as she had told him on the phone, but her face lit up when she noticed him coming around the corner. He stopped beside her and rolled down the passenger window, saying, "Hey, baby. You're a sight for sore eyes."

The relief on her face he was finally here couldn't be more apparent. "Am I glad to see you," she said, opening the cab door and climbing in. "Take me home, honey. I just want to be next to you for the rest of the night."

As he smiled at her, he realized he couldn't have loved this woman more if God would have given him two hearts. The question was, was he betraying her by not telling her what happened, or protecting her? *It won't be for long, remember?* In a few more weeks, this would all be behind them, and he'd tell her everything.

Chapter Seven

It was coming.

The certainty of another death hung in the musky air of this darkened room like a hatchet waiting to fall. Although Jenna was aware of her sleeping state, and she had no idea how she ended up here, she realized the terrified woman screaming bloody murder just outside the dwelling would soon be forced in here with her.

The door burst open, and sparse fragments of moonlight drifted in through the breach. The silhouette of two people spilled in from the doorway. A struggle for life and death ensued between them.

"No! no! no!" a woman's voice wailed, as loud thumping and crashing echoed throughout the place.

"Shut the fuck up!" a man shouted as the female continued to scream and fight back with everything she had.

A sickening *whack!* brought the victim's defensive cries to an end. The dead silence that followed was enough to send a thousand bolts of panic rising through Jenna's chest. *Jesus Christ! Did he kill her?*

A thud reverberated. Something hit the floor. Everything in her gut told her it was the weapon the monster used to strike a death blow to the woman.

Floorboards creaked, penetrating the quietness like the stealth movements of a burglar breaking into a house in the dead of night. The dark figure knelt beside the motionless girl, a move Jenna was certain had been meant to check if the victim survived the assault.

After a few moments suspended in time, commotion once again stirred from the attacker, as he stepped around to the foot of what Jenna assumed was a dead body lying on the floor and lifted its leg. He dragged the woman across the floor, advancing out of eyesight.

Jenna bolted up in bed with a loud gasp. Tears streamed down her cheeks, and she covered her face, softly sobbing. *Oh my God, it's happening all over again.*

Cole was up and reaching for her. "Honey, what's wrong?"

"I don't know," she whispered in the darkness. "But something terrible is happening, Cole."

He sat up in bed and snapped on the lamp.

When she removed her hands and peered over at him, he was staring at her, concern pinching the contours of his face. "Another dream?"

She peered down, not saying anything.

He gathered her in his arms, rubbing her shoulder. "Was it the same one as last time?"

Resting against his chest, she shook her head. "There's someone out there killing women."

He didn't respond.

She got up, wandered over to the armchair, and slowly sat down. "I can't believe this is happening again."

Cole wrestled out from beneath the covers and slid to the end of the bed, sitting up with his legs dangling over. "Talk to me, Jenna?"

She studied him, sleepy eyed and disheveled hair,

and realized in one disheartening moment it didn't matter what she said to him. He wouldn't take it seriously…again.

"It won't make a difference," she said, getting up and heading into the bathroom.

When Jenna reappeared, Cole was no longer sitting on the bed. In fact, he wasn't anywhere in the room.

Stepping into the kitchen, she found him fully dressed, standing over the coffee pot, and taking a sip from the mug in his hand. He turned, noticing her slouched against the frame of the entrance. "You want a cup?"

"Not really."

As he stared at her, she could see anger brewing just below the surface. "What did you mean back there by saying it wouldn't make a difference?"

She strolled into the room, taking a seat at the table. "You won't take me seriously. I could see it in your eyes."

"Is that so?" he said, between clenched teeth. He turned completely around to face her, his back to the counter, and the expression in his eyes leaving no doubt he wasn't the least bit happy with her. "How do you know when you haven't even given me a chance?"

"Do you remember last time? You thought I was full of it. And looking at you a minute ago in the bedroom I could tell what you were thinking."

"This isn't last time, is it? You know as well as I do, a lot has happened since then."

"Okay," she said, standing up and coming toward him, the heat of anger rising in her cheeks. "I saw a man viciously kill a woman. I can't identify either one of them just like before. And I can't even give you a location where the murder took place, only it was in a dark house. Now, tell me, what are you going to do about it?"

He appeared as stunned as if she'd told him his pants were on fire. After setting the mug on the counter, he cleared his throat and said, "The last time you had a dream like this, nothing happened, Jenna. You went to see the professor who told you it was most likely a symbolic dream. We talked about this, remember? You even told me yourself you were under so much stress it was completely possible that's what caused the nightmare."

"Nightmare?" She glared at him in disbelief. "God, I wish it was so. If it were just a nightmare, I could wake up knowing nothing bad was going to happen. People don't die from someone else's nightmare!"

He put his hand on his hip, sighed, and shook his head. "Okay, so bad choice of words. I know you've had visions, honey, and I realize—"

"Don't insult me by treating me like one of your ditsy ex-girlfriends."

His face took on the expression of someone who had just been slapped. "What the hell is that supposed to mean?"

You know what it means."

"The hell I do."

"I'm not stupid, Cole. Why did you leave me stranded at the mechanic shop while you went galivanting around The Vine of McKinney with your ex-lover? You didn't even call me when you damn well knew I had been trying to get in touch with you."

"What? Ava had my phone. I told you."

"I called you so many times there's no way she

wouldn't have heard it ringing if she'd had it."

"Are you calling me a liar?"

As Jenna stared into his eyes, an emotion flickered deep within them. Was that guilt hiding there? "So, I should have called you when I got my phone back," he admitted, glancing away. "But I thought you'd be upset if I didn't book the venue. I had a narrow window of opportunity to get that done before someone else took it. What would you have had me do?"

She didn't really believe he'd cheated on her with Ava, did she? She might have been a little jealous and that was where this little outburst must have come from, but the suspicion he would have done that to her rang hollow, didn't it?

Of course, it did. After all, it had been her idea to use Ava as their wedding planner. Truth be told, Cole hadn't seemed too keen on the idea. Now, the regret of making that decision weighed down on her. This whole thing...her jealousy and ridiculous suspicions could have been avoided if she hadn't felt the need to give someone a second chance. Why did it always have to come down to her being the one made to suffer by trying to do good for others?

But her mistake certainly didn't excuse him from not trusting her enough to know the difference between a dream and a psychic vision. She'd gone through this with him the last time, and he hadn't believed her until he'd seen undeniable proof.

"To answer your question, Cole Rainwater," she said, backing away from him, "I'd have you trust me. That's what I'd have you do. But you don't. And I'm tired of trying to prove myself to you."

As she stormed off, he called out to her, "Jenna.

C'mon. Don't be like this."

****

Jenna sat behind her desk at the office, feeling every bit as big as a grasshopper for how she'd treated Cole this morning. They hardly said two words to each other on the drive here. She should have never accused him of cheating like that. He was not responsible for her foolish emotions of jealousy.

She'd done this to herself by hiring his ex-girlfriend to plan their wedding. How much of an idiot does a girl have to be to have the nerve to think doing what she did would not come without consequences? For all her convictions she'd prove to Cole she wasn't jealous, and she was secure in their relationship, she'd proven the exact opposite to herself. Jenna Langley was no saint. And neither was she beyond the human emotion of envy when it came to her fiancé spending unsupervised time with his ex-lover. It was high time to put a stop to this.

She recalled telling Barbara if she didn't like the way things were going with Ava as their wedding planner, she'd call it off. The time had come to make that phone call and fire Ava Kingsley. But as she grabbed her cell and searched through the contacts for her number, she wasn't completely ready to forgive Cole either. There was still the matter of him not taking her seriously concerning the vision she'd recently had. She was still so shaken up by the clairvoyant episode, her stomach had been in knots all morning. Her hands were tied. Nothing could be done for the girl she'd witnessed being bludgeoned last night. And what was as equally disturbing, was her fiancé thought it was just another dream.

After placing the call, Ava's phone went to voicemail. Jenna left her a quick message to get in touch. Now, all that could be done was to wait.

Her phone rang, and she answered quickly, assuming it was Ava. Time to get this over with. "Listen," she said, taking a deep breath. "I know hiring you as our wedding planner was well intentioned, but it's just not—"

"Ms. Langley," a man, sounding confused, said.

"I'm sorry. Who is this?"

"Brian, at Oasis Auto Repair."

"Oh gosh, I thought you were someone else."

"That's okay. I was calling to let you know your car is fixed and ready to pick up."

"Great. What was wrong with it?"

"That's the strange part. How many enemies do you have?"

Okay, that was an odd question. "I'm not sure what you mean."

"Someone put sugar in your gas tank."

"What? Who would do that?"

"That's not a question I can answer."

"How do you know?"

"Because we couldn't figure out what was the culprit until we pulled the gas tank. That's when we found it."

"Are you sure that's what it was?"

"Positive."

Holy shit. She could think of no one who would purposely do that. Perhaps it was some unruly kids playing a prank.

"The good news is the car is running great now. When do you think you can swing by and get it?"

"Um. Let me work on that. Can you give me about an hour?"

"Sure. It'll be here."

As she got off the phone, her mind wandered to a thousand different reasons why sugar could have ended up in her gas tank. She had no enemies to speak of, or at least none she was aware of. School was out for summer, and every time she'd left the office, she'd spotted kids riding their bikes up and down the roads. One of them, or a group of them probably thought it would be hilarious to pull a prank like that on some unsuspecting person. No other scenario made a bit of sense. Now, she had no idea where she could park her car to keep the same thing from happening again.

She should call Cole, then she thought better of it. She was still upset with him. *Don't be an idiot. He's still your soon-to-be-husband whether you're pissed at him or not. He needs to know about your car.*

She searched for his number against her better judgement and dialed it. When he answered, he said, "Are you still mad at me?"

"Yes."

"Then why are you calling?"

She didn't like his surly tone. Two could play that game. "I heard from the mechanic and thought you'd want to know about the car."

"I'm listening."

He was being an ass, and she fought the urge to simply hang up on him. But she wasn't a child like he was. "It's fixed, but they said someone put sugar in the gas tank."

"Are you sure?"

"That's what they said."

"Do you want me to come get you? We can go pick it up."

"Don't bother," she said, "I'll call Barb. Have a nice day."

"Jenna," he said, right before she took the phone away and ended the call.

The device rang again. It was him.

She ignored it, deciding in the heat of the moment she was a bigger child than him after all. Let him stew in his crappy attitude for a while.

She rang Barbara. When her best friend answered, she said, "I need a favor. Can you take me to the mechanic shop to pick up my car?"

"Where's Cole?"

"Stuck in an elevator for all I care."

"Uh oh, what happened?"

"I don't want to talk about it. Just please. Can you take me or not?"

"Okay, okay. Are you at the office?"

"I'm still here."

"I'll be there in fifteen minutes."

"Thank you. And Barb?"

"Yes."

"I'm asking you not to be nosy just this once. I don't want to talk about what's going on between me and Cole, okay?"

"I won't ask, I promise."

She closed her eyes as the first teardrops rolled down her face. She couldn't have been more appreciative her best friend got the message for once in her life. While on the phone with Cole she wanted nothing more than to break down, apologize, and tell him how much she loved him. The pain of not being on good terms with the man who meant everything in the world to her was the worst agony imaginable. But she could no longer sit by and passively watch while he dismissed her clairvoyant abilities. After all they'd gone through with the murder victims of his father, she'd have figured he would have learned to trust her premonitions by now. But, somehow, they were right back at square one. And she just couldn't reconcile with allowing it to go on. Visions were part of who she was, and if he couldn't accept that, she didn't know how stable a future they could ever have together. If it weren't confronted now, it would just keep coming up every time they'd have a disagreement.

"See you when you get here." Once she laid the phone down, the torture she'd held in since the explosion with Cole this morning poured out of her like water bursting over a damn. And she wept alone in her office with no one to see.

****

That rotten bitch was the cause of this.

Red-hot anger billowed through Cole like smoke pouring out of a chimney. Ava Kingsley put sugar in Jenna's gas tank, and he was as sure of that as he had been about anything in his life. She'd done it to prevent Jenna from going to the venue. The kiss she planted on him was no impulse like she claimed. She had set him up from the very beginning. All of it had been orchestrated to either get him alone because she'd never gotten over their love affair, or to get revenge on him by causing a rift between him and his fiancée because he'd dumped her.

Either way, he'd be damned if she'd get away with it.

He picked up his phone and dialed her number. She answered on the third ring. "Hello."

"We need to meet right now. Where are you?"

She breathed heavily, then said, "I can meet in ten minutes. What's this about?"

"I'll be at the coffee shop on the corner of White and Fifth."

He ended the call, not giving her an opportunity to say another word. He'd get to the bottom of this all right by putting his detective skills to work. He was going to look her squarely in the eyes and pointedly accuse her of the dirty deed he already knew she was guilty of committing. Then he'd sit back and observe her reaction. A person's body language spoke louder than any line of bullshit coming out of their mouths. He had been trained how to spot a lie a mile away. This time he was going to be the one in control though.

Cole snatched up his keys, stopped by Gibbs' office to say he had an errand to run, and marched to his truck with purposeful strides.

Approaching the coffee shop, he spotted her apple-red sports car parked at the front of the establishment. He parked beside it, got out, and stalked into the place as if he owned it. She sat at a table in the corner, her back turned to him. He approached without saying a word and planted himself in the chair across from her.

She opened her mouth to say something, and he shut her down quick as lightning. "Someone put something in Jenna's gas tank yesterday. Do you know anything about that?"

The brief second her attention cut away he became confident she was guilty.

She bounded back quickly, though, feigning shock.

"Of course, I don't. Why would you ask me that?"

"Because you did it."

The expression in her eyes reflected confusion, and then deep anguish. "I can't believe you think I'd do something like that."

Oh, she was good.

But he was better.

"Oh, I know you did it. But I'm not exactly sure why. Is it because I broke it off with you? Maybe you couldn't stand to see me happy. Is that it?"

"You're crazy."

"I'm resourceful. You're the one who's batshit crazy, lady. You played on my fiancée's sympathies to hire you to plan our wedding. You planted yourself in a position where you could do the most damage. What was your motive?" He frowned, giving off the impression it was no big deal. "You can tell me. I already know you're guilty. Why'd you do it, Ava?"

"Anyone could have put sugar in her gas tank. Why are you insisting it was me?"

Satisfaction reeled through him. "Well," he said, with a condescending smile, "for starters, I said someone put *something* in Jenna's gas tank, I never mentioned what that something was."

Fear gripped her features with the swiftness of a serpent's strike. She glanced away quickly, almost in a blind panic to find an acceptable rebound. "It...it's common sense if someone put something in her gas tank, it was most likely sugar."

He was breaking down her carefully constructed façade. Her face trembled, and nervousness caused her to swallow hard. Cracks were forming, and it was time to move in for the kill.

He grabbed her arm in a quick motion and applied enough pressure to deliver just the shock factor he needed. Then he held her prisoner with a fiery gaze, and leaned across the table, a hairsbreadth from her. "You were angry at me for leaving you. I don't blame you. If someone did that to me, I would have been pissed too." It was a clever tactic he'd learned as a homicide detective to get suspects to confess the truth. Apply enough pressure on the subject while simultaneously sympathizing with them.

It appeared to be working. He could tell her heartrate picked up by the flush in her checks, and the weakness in her eyes grew leaps and bounds. "I can understand why you would be upset with me, even want to get even," he said, keeping up with the tension. "I hurt you and it wasn't fair."

"I…I…never meant to…to—"

Glass shattered in the distance, and Ava's head snapped around as a man knelt to pick up pieces of a broken saucer on the floor. The guy glanced over at them and shrugged. "Sorry."

When she drew her attention back to Cole, he could tell the control had returned to her face. "Let go of me," she said, wrestling with his grip on her arm.

He tightened his hold on her, jerking her forward. When she was a mere inch from his face, he whispered, "If you continue to fuck with me and my fiancée, sweetheart, you're going to get hurt worse than when I kicked your sorry ass to the curb. Got it?" He released her arm, and stood, towering over her pathetic form. "You can consider yourself fired."

He stormed out with a resolute determination to go see Jenna and tell her everything Ava had done. There was no way in hell that bitch in there was going to stand in the way of him and his soon-to-be-wife's happiness.

****

Upon returning to the office after Barb took her to get her car, Jenna plopped down into the chair behind the desk. The distraction of going to the mechanic shop allowed her a little time to cool off. It gave her an opportunity to think more level-headed about the issue between her and Cole. Perhaps, she should attempt to sit down with him in a calm manner and explain how his dismissal of her visions upset her.

The full-blown argument they had gotten into this morning, coupled with her jealousy of Ava made it impossible for the two of them to have a meaningful discussion about what truly bothered her. Before she'd throw up her hands and admit defeat, she at least owed him a calm and collected explanation of what he'd done that made her so distraught.

Her phone rang. Barb was calling. She picked it up finally ready to talk to her best friend about the trouble between her and Cole. "Hey," she said, much more composed than she had been ten minutes ago.

After waiting thirty seconds for her friend to respond, Jenna said, "You there?"

"I'm here."

"Is everything all right?"

"I don't know."

"Okay, you're going to have to give me more than that."

"I just saw Cole leaving the coffee shop up the road. Ava came out soon after he pulled off."

Jenna's breath caught in her throat. "What are you saying?"

"I'm saying what I'm saying. Was he supposed to meet Ava this morning?"

"Are you sure it was Cole and Ava you saw?"

"I know what they look like."

Jenna reflected on the short conversation with Cole when she'd called him about the car. He didn't say anything about meeting with Ava. Of course, she'd hardly said ten words to him before hanging up. But things were fine between them last night, and he'd mentioned nothing about the need to get together with Ava then. What was going on here?

The express mail delivery man strolled through her office door, standing in front of the desk with a large envelope in his hand. She wasn't expecting any packages.

"Listen, Barbara, let me call you right back. Someone just came into the office."

"Okay, but don't forget about me."

As she laid her phone down, the delivery man handed out the envelope, saying, "I'll need you to sign for this."

She took the package from him and studied the return address. It came from a few towns over. The sender was a private detective firm. She didn't recognize the name.

With her interest piqued, she set it aside and took the signature form from the guy.

The minute he strolled out, she tore into it, drawing out the contents. What her eyes glossed across caused a sharp gasp. The items slipped from her grasp and fell to the desk.

****

Cole's heart was in his throat when he swung his

truck into the parking lot of Jenna's office. He imagined she would be a little peeved when he told her about Ava's kiss and explained why he didn't mention it last night. But once she realized the psychopath put sugar in her gas tank to keep her away from the venue long enough to put her devious plan in place to form a wedge between them, her anger would rightfully focus on the source of their anguish. And it wasn't him.

He got out of the truck, taking a deep breath, and facing the office. It was time to march in there and set things right. The moment he shuffled through the door, Jenna stood there, her eyes fresh with tears as she stared at something on her desk.

He approached, noticing a large, torn envelope lying there, and two eight-by-ten photos sitting side by side.

She finally peered up at him and his attention fell to the pictures.

Disbelief slammed through him as he gazed at him and Ava holding hands on the concrete steps of the venue. He recognized it as when she'd grabbed his hand, giving him the phone, and closing his fingers around it.

It got worse when he studied the second photo. Of course, it was the kiss.

"Oh, no, no, no. This is not what you think," he insisted, fire engulfing him.

The pained expression etched into her face when she picked up the photos and sent them flying against his chest was like a dagger to the heart. "You son-of-a-bitch!" she wailed. "How could you do this to me?"

Cole quickly shuffled around the desk and took her by the arms. "Jenna. Listen to me. This was Ava's doing. She set us up. That picture of us holding hands was when she grabbed my hand and slipped me my phone. I didn't even know she had it. She just walked up and took my hand."

"What about that?" She stabbed a finger at the picture laying on the floor on the opposite side of the desk of the two of them kissing.

"As we were leaving the venue, she walked up and kissed me, Jenna. I was surprised as hell. We got into a huge argument about it."

She wiggled out of his hold, her expression not buying it. "Then why didn't you tell me? If she kissed you without your permission, you had plenty of time to tell me, didn't you? But all last night and again this morning, you said nothing about it."

"Dammit, Jenna. I wanted to tell you. You have no idea how keeping that from you has been eating me up inside. I felt so guilty for not being honest with you. But I knew how stressed you've been, and how relieved you were when you finally found someone to help you with the wedding. I was torn between telling you the truth now and having you worry like that again or keeping my distance from Ava and telling you after the wedding. At least that would have spared you the anxiety of trying to plan our wedding with no one to help you."

She appeared incredulous. "And you think knowing what I know now, I would have wanted that unscrupulous woman to help plan our wedding? Do you really think it would have made a difference if you'd told me after? It would have only angered me more, knowing you let me think everything was fine, while I let that bitch plan our wedding."

He lowered his head, words evading him. She was right. He had been so caught up thinking the assault had been committed against him, and he could handle keeping it under wraps to save her from dealing with added stress, it never occurred to him she was a target also. "I'm sorry, honey. I should have told you like I wanted to all along, and not been so obsessed with worrying about how it was going to affect you."

Her eyes softened for a fleeting moment, and then it vanished like the passing wind. She took a step back, leveling him with a glower of renewed anger and jealousy. "At this point, I can't even be sure the kiss wasn't mutual. You say it wasn't. But how do I know that?"

Look at those pictures," he said, pointing to them. "Why would she send those to you? What do you think she's trying to accomplish by doing that? She's the one who put sugar in your gas tank to keep you away from the venue. She planned on forcing that kiss on me, all while she'd hired someone, probably a PI, to snap photographs in the background."

Jenna glanced at the envelope on the desk.

The action wasn't lost on Cole, and he snatched it up, examining the name on the label. "That's what I thought," he said, tossing the damned thing back on the desk. "This came from the office of a PI. Hell, I'm even familiar with the firm she used for this little charade for Christ's sake."

"Then tell me, what were you doing with her at the coffee shop up the road," Jenna said, pointing toward the window behind him.

"When you told me earlier someone put sugar in your gas tank, I knew exactly who did it. Doesn't it seem a little too convenient how you couldn't make it to the venue due to car trouble, the same venue she just happened to force a kiss on me at? When I got off the phone with you, I called her and told her to meet me there. I went there to confront her, Jenna. How do you know about that anyhow?"

"It damn sure wasn't because you told me, Cole. It appears there's a lot of things you don't tell me."

"So, who did?"

"Barbara saw the both of you leaving together."

"The hell she did," he said, hot anger swelling inside him. "Ava was still sitting in the coffee shop when I walked out. So, now Barb is lying to you?"

Jenna glared at him as if he had some nerve to accuse her best friend of anything unholy. "Barbara said Ava walked out after you drove away."

"That's not the same as leaving together, is it?"

"I don't see where it matters. You were there with her."

"And I just told you why!"

"So, tell me why again, you neglected to call me yesterday, even after Ava returned your phone and told you I was waiting for you to call me."

Cole exhaled in frustration. "She didn't tell me that. She told me you realized you probably wouldn't make it. And you wanted us to go in and handle things."

Jenna was blown away. "That's not at all what I told her. I said to please let you know I had been trying to get in touch with you, and to have you call me back as soon as she saw you."

He frowned, nodding in a gesture of I told you so. "Why does that not surprise me. Can't you see she's playing us? This whole thing is nothing more than a huge trap, her way of getting revenge on me for ending things with her. She hated to see us happy together."

"Even if it was, Cole. We made a promise to one another we would always tell each other the truth. We made a vow to never hide things from each other, remember? Knowing that, you made a clear decision to hide from me the fact she kissed you."

"I know. And as much as I'd give anything to take back that decision, it's not within my power to do that. But I regret it more than you'll ever know." He stared into her eyes, willing her to believe him.

She lowered her head, shaking it. "It's not just that," she whispered. "You don't trust my intuitions."

"If this is about your dream, Jenna—"

"It wasn't a dream," she snapped back. "Even after all this time, you still don't take me seriously when I tell you I've had a vision."

"The last time you had a vision, nothing happened. I just think—"

"We need a little time to think about what we're doing here."

He glared at her, eyes burning with disbelief. "What are you saying?"

Her attention danced around him. "I'm just saying I think we need to work some things out before we…"

"Get married?" He couldn't believe what she was insinuating.

"I think so."

"So, you're calling off the wedding?"

She still refused to glance at him. "I'm just—"

"Calling off the wedding, aren't you?"

Jenna finally threw a stare in his direction, hurt

reflecting in her eyes. "It wouldn't be right to get married until we've had a chance to work everything out."

"Then, let's work it out. Right here and now." He sat down on the corner of the desk, folding his hands in his lap. "I'm here, and I'm listening."

"Okay, when do you plan to look into the death I witnessed this morning?"

Her words stunned him. "How can I do that when I don't have enough details to even launch an investigation?"

"If I would have been able to provide more details, would you have opened an investigation?"

He sat there, having nothing to offer, or at least nothing he was sure she'd want to hear.

"Let me answer for you. You wouldn't because you don't trust my visions. Even after several people died the last time, you still question whether or not what I see is real."

When he still had no response, she said, "I want you to leave, please."

He lunged off the desk, hardly believing how drastically the tide had turned for them. "C'mon, Jenna, I—"

"Just go."

Her tone told him this wasn't up for discussion. He had a sinking feeling the rocky road they just hit might be their undoing. But he couldn't control how unreasonable she was being. How could she realistically expect him to open a murder investigation when there wasn't a bit of tangible evidence to justify it? They'd laugh him out of the precinct. Surely, she had enough common sense to realize that. But studying her right now, it appeared she couldn't care less about it. "I'm sorry you feel this way," he said, rising to his feet, collecting the two photos scattered on the floor, and heading toward the door. He peered back at her before exiting. "We could have worked this out," he said, heart in his throat. "But you're too hell-bent on letting Ava win."

****

Cole trudged into Sara's Wedding Planning Services doggedly determined to get some straight answers from Ava as to why she hired a PI to take pictures of them and have the guy mail them to Jenna.

He stopped at the only desk that had a person sitting behind it. "Where's Ava Kingsley?" he asked, gruffly, knowing the expression on his face must have been dark and hostile. But he didn't care.

The woman just sat there, staring at him as if she had no clue what to say.

He pressed. "She works here, doesn't she?"

"Yes, she does," another lady answered, striding over to him. "But she's not in right now. Is there something one of us can help you with?"

Cole examined the newcomer through narrowed eyes. She had an air of superiority about her. "Are you the owner?"

She nodded. "You seem a little upset, Mr.—"

"Rainwater," he provided.

Now the woman behind the desk spoke up. "Oh, this is the couple Ava is working with. Jenna Langley and Cole Rainwater."

"*Was* working with," Cole corrected.

The owner's brows furrowed. "I would ask if everything's all right, but from the look on your face, I can see it isn't. Can you tell me what happened?"

"This happened," he said, tossing the photos of him and Ava on the desk.

Both women leaned over to get a better view, and when the owner peered up again, surprise lit her face.

Cole cleared his throat. "Ava put sugar in my fiancée's gas tank to keep her from joining us at the venue she'd scheduled us to tour. She kissed me as we were leaving and hired a PI to take those pictures, then had them mailed to my fiancée's place of business."

A gasp bellowed out from the woman behind the desk. When Cole peered at her, she had her hand to her mouth, in a state of complete shock. As soon as she removed her hand, she said, "I heard Ava and Ms. Langley arguing outside in the parking lot the day she came here. I couldn't hear what was said, but Ms. Langley seemed pretty upset when she stormed out of here."

Cole reflected on the conversation he and Jenna had concerning her shock when she discovered his ex-girlfriend worked at the wedding planner's office. She must have gotten into it with Ava before the sly snake groveled at her feet and made her feel badly enough to hire her, under the guise of giving her a second chance.

"Ava is an ex-girlfriend. I broke it off with her a year ago. She ran into us at a restaurant while we were dining last week and made a spectacle of herself and embarrassed my fiancée. Jenna had no idea she worked here when we got the brochure for your business in the mail. She came here to hire someone to help with our wedding, and Ava made her feel sorry enough for her she decided to give her a second chance. Then she did this," he said, stabbing a finger at the despicable photos.

The owner's expression twisted with confusion. "Pardon me, did you say you received a brochure from our company in the mail?"

"That's what brought Jenna here."

"We don't mail out brochures, Mr. Rainwater."

"That's what I thought, too," the girl behind the desk said. She slid open her desk drawer and fumbled around for a minute. Then she produced a pamphlet and laid it on the desk. She asked Cole, "Is this the brochure you're talking about?"

He poked a finger at it. "That's the one."

"Ms. Langley brought this in with her when she came," the girl added.

"Let me see that." The owner grabbed the brochure and paged through it. When she was done, she stared at Cole. "This brochure is not ours. I don't know where it came from."

The truth hit Cole like a Mack truck. He could not believe how elaborate Ava's scheme was, and how much time and effort she'd put into pulling it off. She had gone so far as to create a brochure and mail it to them, for Christ's sake. But how did she know they would bite on it? Or was she throwing darts at the wall hoping one would hit the bullseye?

That didn't make sense. That day at the restaurant, she couldn't have known whether they had already hired a wedding planner. Unless she took the time to dig into it.

The detective in him kicked in when he grabbed the brochure off the table to use as possible evidence. "When did Ava apply for the job here?"

The girl behind the desk swung into action, rummaging through the file cabinet next to her desk.

She plucked out a document and set it down, then leafed through it, searching for something. She peered up at Cole. "This is Ava's application. According to the date here, she filled this out on the tenth of this month."

That was the day after she'd approached them at the restaurant. He picked up the brochure once more and took a detailed look at it, noticing this time there was no postage stamp on it. Ava didn't mail it out. There wouldn't have been enough time for that. She put the damn thing in his mailbox. She knew exactly what she was doing by applying here, slipping the brochure in his mail, and then when her victim walked through the door, sinking her hooks into her.

But the gig was up. Unfortunately, it may have already accomplished its goal of ripping him and Jenna apart. Why would anyone go to these lengths to get back at an ex-lover? Someone they'd dated for less than three months.

A woman entered the main lobby from the hallway in the back. Her strides were quick and purposeful as she approached the front desk. "Um, Mrs. Harper?"

The owner's attention settled on her. "What is it, Elizabeth?"

"I overheard the conversation so I went back to Ava's office to get the file on the Rainwaters, hoping it would bring clarity to the situation. I noticed Ms. Kingsley has cleared out her desk."

Mrs. Harper took a step back. "What do you mean cleared out her desk?" The owner swung into action, heading toward the hallway in an obvious attempt to check on the state of Ava's office.

The assistant who made the announcement was quick on her heels, saying, "There's nothing on her desk. The file cabinets are empty."

The women's chatter floated down the hallway, as Cole digested what he'd just learned. The fact Ava packed up and left directly after the incident further cemented his suspicion her employment here was nothing more than a means to get at him and Jenna. Something wasn't adding up here. Who would uproot their life and take these drastic measures to get revenge for a love affair gone awry a year ago? There had to be something else, another motive in place, a big chunk of this mystery he was missing. His ex-lover was after something more than revenge.

He collected the brochure and the photos from the desk and nodded a farewell to the pleasant lady sitting behind it.

He had some investigating to do. Right after he made a phone call.

Chapter Eight

Jenna closed the office in the afternoon, too upset to finish out the day after the earlier confrontation with Cole. The phone call with Barb five minutes ago did nothing to make her feel better. Her best friend wasn't one hundred percent on her side where it concerned this issue. She could still hear the woman's reprimand ringing in her ears. *This whole thing was trouble. I could see this coming a mile down the road. I wish you would have just listened.*

She hadn't, now, had she? There was no use crying over spilled milk. She couldn't go back and change it. If Cole had just been honest like he'd promised, instead of hiding an ex-lover's kiss from her, then they could have put a stop to this thing before it got so out-of-hand.

Was he guilty of enjoying the kiss? Is that why he hid it from her? *Just stop it! You're going to drive yourself insane.*

She had no doubt that Cole was right about one thing: that vengeful bitch Ava planned this. Every despicable step of it. The pictures that had been mailed to her office undoubtedly proved that. She had no doubt Ava put sugar in her gas tank to keep her from joining them at the venue, all so she could put her wicked scheme in place to drive them apart.

Was Cole also right about Jenna letting her win? *No way. He doesn't get off that easy.* It was his actions, or inactions, that caused this rift between them, not Ava's. All he had to do was level with her, just as the two of them vowed they would always do, no matter what. If he couldn't hold up his end of that bargain now, what would happen down the road when something else occurred? Would he use the same excuse he didn't want to upset her as the reason why he felt justified in not coming clean with her?

Even though she found herself faltering in her conviction to hold her ground with Cole as she headed across the parking lot, unlocked her car, and slid in, she ultimately decided she couldn't live like that, always worrying if he were telling the truth, and wondering what he could be hiding from her. His inability to accept her clairvoyant gifts only pushed her farther over the edge. If he loved her the way he said he did, he'd be willing to work these things out with her. He'd see how important they were to her.

She had a few necessary business errands to run before closing out the day, and then she'd head to the house and pack a bag. Continuing to stay with him at his place would only give him false assurance his actions didn't matter in their relationship. It would make him think hiding things from her was acceptable, and when the dust settled, she'd just get over it. But in her heart, she realized if he didn't come to terms with his dishonesty toward her, and if he couldn't accept her for who she was, psychic visions and all, they didn't have much hope for the future. But knowing that did not stop the tears from spilling down her cheeks, as she started up the car and drove out of the parking lot. All she wanted to do was go running to him and surrender this fight to the warmth and security of his embrace. It would be so easy…and so reckless.

She found a tissue in the console and dried her eyes. The only hope they had was if he would be willing to see his dishonesty is what caused this grief more than any other factor. Maybe a night away from each other would be all it would take. Her bleeding heart could only hope.

****

Remembering the address of the PI's office he'd spotted on the envelope during the heated argument with Jenna, Cole pointed his truck in that direction while he picked up the phone and dialed Gibbs' number.

His partner answered. "Hey, man, what's up?"

"Listen, I need you to do me a favor."

"Okay…" There was skepticism in Gibbs' voice. "Everything all right?"

"Not really, but I want you to run a name for me. Can you do that?"

"Sure. Want to talk about what's wrong?"

"Maybe another day."

"I don't like the sound of that. But Lord knows how stubborn you are. What's the name?"

"Ava Kingsley."

Silence, and then, "Wait, isn't that—"

"You probably remember her from the Farmersville PD 4th of July party last year. I showed up with her. We were dating at the time."

"And now you want to do a background check on her?"

"That's right."

"Can I ask why?"

"No."

"Okay. What am I looking for here?"

"Priors. Run ins with the police. Anything you can dig up. And I'm going to need her address. I'm not sure if it changed from when I dated her. I just don't have time to run a search right now."

"Do you suspect her of criminal activity?"

"Yup. Unfortunately, nothing I can prove at the moment."

"I'm in the middle of something right now, so give me just a little bit."

"The quicker the better."

"Roger that."

Cole took a right on St. Gemini Street, and Benjamin Private Investigator Firm came into view. He drove into the parking lot and killed the engine. This ought to be an interesting chat between him and Nicholas Benjamin. Cole remembered the guy as being a real shyster. He'd take on any case, no matter the moral standing, if the price were right.

Still fuming from Ava's blatant trickery, he grabbed the pictures the lowlife PI had mailed to Jenna and shuffled out of the truck.

When he entered the office, Nicholas was on the phone. Cole ripped a trail across the floor, loomed over the guy's desk and slammed the photos down. "I suggest you get off the phone. Now."

Surprise flitted across Benjamin's face as he peered at the pictures. He cleared his throat and said to the person on the line, "Hey, Brandon, something just came up. Let me call you back."

"You're damn right it did," Cole sneered, fighting the urge to leap across the desk and throttle the bastard.

"Look, detective. This was nothing personal. I was

just doing what I was hired to do."

"Ava Kingsley put you up to this?"

"I have no idea what you're talking about."

Before he could turn away, Cole leaned over and with one thrust of his hand, snatched the guy around the throat. "Answer the question."

Benjamin thrashed about, knocking several items off his desk and sending them crashing to the floor. He clawed at the fist around his neck, but Cole only tightened the chokehold.

When the man's face took on a purple hue, he released him.

The PI dropped into the chair, gasping for air, eyes bulging. When he finally got control of his faculties, anger and shock emanated from him. "What do you think you're doing? How dare you barge into my office and—"

Cole lunged toward him again, and the guy cringed, throwing his hands up. "All right, all right, I have no idea who Ava Kingsley is. That's not the name of the person who hired me to take those pictures."

Cole narrowed his eyes on the PI. Who else could it have been if not Ava?

"It was some guy named Isaac Driscoll."

Was Ava working with someone? How deep did this thing go? "Describe what he looks like."

"I don't know. I never saw him. He called my office and hired me to be at The Vine of McKinney by four o'clock yesterday. I was instructed to wait in the parking lot and take pictures of you and another woman in a compromising position. And then mail the photos to your fiancée's office."

"And you never questioned why?" This kind of

behavior was typical of Nicholas Benjamin. Everyone in investigative circles knew the man was not interested in gritty PI work. He was much more intrigued by the size of his client's purse strings, and he'd do anything for a good payout.

"I don't get paid to ask why."

"How much did he pay you to set me up?"

"Look, it isn't my place to—"

"How much?"

"Five-thousand dollars."

Cole grinned snidely. "Is that the going rate for destroying someone's life? You're selling out cheap, aren't you? I would have charged at least double."

For the first time, he caught a glimpse of remorse in the man's expression. But it was short lived as his attention shifted, and then settled on Cole once more with a renewed sense of self-importance. "Are you finished with me, detective?"

"Not quite. How did Mr. Driscoll pay you?"

"By credit card over the phone."

"I'll need a copy of that transaction."

"I'm not giving my client's credit card information to you."

Cole grabbed his badge, and held it out, saying, "Then I'll be more than happy to arrest you for impeding with a police investigation."

Nicholas stood up, enraged. "You can't do that."

"Sit back down, Mr. Benjamin," he ordered. The threatening disposition rolling off him swayed the PI into compliance. As the man retook his seat, Cole said, "This is a criminal investigation. So, I'm going to ask one more time for the transaction history."

"What crime was committed?" Benjamin asked, his

expression incredulous.

"Someone put sugar in my fiancée's gas tank. That's a crime."

"What? I don't know anything about that. I certainly don't see what that has to do with me."

"Because whoever committed the crime did it to keep my fiancée from attending the tour of the venue with me and the wedding planner, Ava Kingsley. Then they hired you to snap photos of Ms. Kingsley coming on to me, and had you mail those pictures to my fiancée's place of business."

For once, the man appeared clueless. "Why would someone do that?"

"They used you, Mr. Benjamin. As a means with which to commit their crime. But of course, that could have been prevented if you'd deployed your investigative skills for more than a front to collect cash and asked questions like a real PI."

The man lowered his head, appearing to realize at last the seriousness of the situation. "Okay" he said, shaking his head. "I'll get the information you want." He rolled the mouse around the mouse pad for a minute, then the printer sprang to life.

Benjamin leaned over and snatched the page that had just printed, handing it to Cole, saying, "Here's the transaction information. Now, please just leave."

****

Cole's phone rang as he shut himself inside the truck. He was glad to see Gibbs' contact pop up. "What'd you find," he asked, relieved his partner was able to run the search so quickly.

"Not much. Ava Kingsley came up clean as a whistle. I found a few minor traffic violations over the years, but other than that…"

For some reason, the fact she had a clean record didn't surprise him. He just discovered there was a second person involved. And he'd bet his millions her co-partner in crime would be the one with the criminal history. "Do you have her address?"

"Yeah. Looks like she's lived in the same place for a few years now. It's a small house in McKinney off Pine Road."

It was the same address Cole remembered. "I have another name I need you to run."

"Okay. Now I'm going to have to ask why."

Cole sighed, knowing he couldn't have kept Gibbs at bay for much longer. He'd have to start from the beginning. When he finished rattling off the bizarre events of the last few days, his partner exhaled, and said, "So, you think Ava Kingsley, or this guy, Isaac Driscoll was the one who put sugar in Jenna's gas tank?"

"Don't you?"

"You'd have a hard time proving that, but it is definitely likely."

"Listen, I realize we don't have enough here to launch a formal investigation. But something fishy is going on. Even if Ava was jealous of my relationship with Jenna, it doesn't make sense for her to go to these drastic measures to split us up. There is something more to this. And I'd bet Isaac Driscoll holds the key. Just run the guy's name. Let's see what comes up. I'm about to head to Ava's place. Maybe I'll get lucky and catch her there. She stopped answering my phone calls."

"What do you plan to do if you see her?"

"Get the truth out of her one way or the other. I had

her close to confessing at the coffee shop this morning. I know with a little more goading, I can drag it out of her."

"All right. I'll catch up with you when I have something to report."

Cole drove out of the parking lot and headed toward Pine Road considering all that had transpired so far with a little investigative action. What exactly was Ava up to? At this point he realized a simple motive to break him and Jenna up couldn't be the end-prize. Under the surface there was something more she had to have been getting out of this other than the satisfaction of feeding her supposed revenge. They only dated for a few months and that was a year ago. If some weird obsession she'd acquired for him had been the culprit all along, surely, he would have heard from her before now. She would have made her presence known not long after he broke it off with her, and she wouldn't have accepted the end to their relationship so gracefully. She'd gone so far as to get hired on for a position she had no plans to keep and solicited the help of someone else to pull this farce off. Or perhaps, someone solicited her. Maybe this Isaac Driscoll was a criminal Cole helped put away, and the guy was out of prison and looking for revenge. But what would Ava get out of helping him? Unless they were lovers.

Cole racked his brain to awaken some memory of past dealings with a guy named Isaac Driscoll. But there was nothing. It would be interesting to see what Gibbs was able to come up with. Until then, he'd track Ava down, and when he found her, she'd damn well talk. She'd finish telling him what she started to spill at the coffee shop.

He drove into a familiar neighborhood. If memory served correct, the dwelling Ava lived in was a small, twelve-hundred square foot place a few houses down from here. He spotted it on the right and slowed the truck as he approached. The tulip bed was still in the front yard. The familiar manicured shrubs lined both sides of the walkway leading to the front steps. And he recognized the yellow swing hanging from the front porch. He didn't see a vehicle in the driveway, but the garage was closed.

He parked the truck along the side of the road and got out, wandering up the walkway. He stood in front of the door hitting the buzzer. Nothing. He knocked loudly. Still no answer, and no movements coming from inside. Then he tested the doorknob and discovered it was unlocked.

Before he could talk himself out of it, he twisted the knob, forcing the door open. He cautiously stepped into an empty hallway. His footfalls, as he advanced further into the house, echoed throughout the place.

Then he took the corner, staring at an empty living room. There was not a single stick of furniture to be had. No decorations hanging from the wall, only discolored shapes where pictures once covered those spots. He stepped over to the light switch and flipped it on. Nothing happened.

With a disturbing realization settling in his gut, he rushed over to the kitchen and twisted the knob to the faucet. Nothing came out of it.

He searched the rest of the rooms, already knowing she'd packed up and left. When he hiked back to the front door, he couldn't believe what his eyes were seeing. It appeared she'd abandoned her home just as quickly as she had abandoned her job. What was she running from? Then it occurred to him perhaps Gibbs did not have her current address. Could she have moved out at a much earlier date? But when he'd wandered outside, he noticed the grass had been cut, and everything appeared well manicured. Yet, if she had moved out previously, the landlord would have kept the place up for prospective renters.

As he made his way to the truck, the sound of a weed-eater starting up caught his attention. He peered over to catch a glimpse of the neighbor trimming weeds around the front of his house. "Excuse me," he hollered, getting the man's attention.

The guy switched off the contraption and stared at him expectantly.

"Can you tell me if Ava Kingsley still lives here?"

"She did. But some guys with a moving truck took the rest of her belongings out yesterday."

"Did she happen to tell you where she was going?"

The neighbor shrugged, appearing puzzled. "I didn't even know she was leaving."

She hightailed it out of here. But why, was the nagging question.

"Thanks," Cole said.

The guy nodded and fired up his weed-eater again.

As Cole climbed into the truck, the pressure was building to find out why she'd left so quickly. Whatever the reason, something was coming. Something she was hoping to outrun.

He got on the phone with Gibbs as he drove off. The words bursting from him in a rushed litany. "Ava no longer lives here. Movers took the rest of her stuff yesterday. She's running from something, Gibbs."

"I think you're right. Any idea what?"

"I get the feeling it's something big. And I think it involves me and Jenna."

"You're not going to believe what I found on Driscoll."

"What?"

"The guy is from Richland Hills. He reported his wallet stolen a few days ago."

"You're kidding."

"He thinks it was lifted while he was at the Cadillac Bar."

Cole was hopeful. "I wonder if the place has cameras."

"I already called. They do, but they have been out of commission for a few weeks now."

"Dammit. Maybe I should ride over there and talk to the staff."

"I questioned the manager while I was on the phone with her. The place was crawling with customers on the night Driscoll thinks his wallet was stolen. It would be a longshot, and probably not worth your time."

"Any possibility Driscoll is using the excuse his wallet was stolen as a cover?"

"He made a report."

"I get that. But anyone can report a wallet stolen. If he's the guilty party, he could have planned for this ahead of time to cover his tracks in the event we tracked him down to the PI's office."

"I think you're reaching on this one, brother. I talked to the guy. He's a security guard. I don't see a connection and didn't sense he was trying to hide anything. His record is squeaky clean."

Cole sighed. "You're probably right."

"Here's my feeling on this. Whoever called Benjamin's office purposely stole Driscoll's wallet to use his credit card to pay for the services. Obviously, he couldn't use his own name and payment method because of what you said. We'd be able to track him, and he needed to avoid that."

"I'm really feeling the heat to find out who the son-of-a-bitch behind this is, and what his connection is to Ava, who is in this up to her bloody neck."

"I get it. But don't let impatience interfere with your investigation sense. That only leads down a road to nowhere fast. You know that."

Gibbs was right. He couldn't let that happen. It was easy for a detective to get caught up in that web. Let the case tell the story. Don't try to import your story into the case.

"What are you going to do now?" Gibbs wanted to know.

"I've run out of leads. Not sure what I can do."

"You know the drill. Give it some time. Another one will tumble into your lap."

"That's the problem. I don't know how much time I have before this thing rears its head."

"What do you think is going to happen?"

He took the highway ramp, heading in the direction of his house to see if Jenna was there since she wasn't answering his calls, and the last time he'd driven past her office, her car wasn't in the parking lot. "I don't know. But something's coming. I can feel it in my bones. Ava wouldn't just pick up and leave without a trace like that. I don't know if she's the mastermind behind this, or if the guy who paid Benjamin to take those photos is." He took a deep breath and then admitted, "Jenna's been having dreams again."

"What kind of dreams?"

"It's part of the reason she won't talk to me right now. I didn't take her seriously. I blew it again. Can you believe that."

"Maybe you're being too hard on yourself."

He shook his head, damn well knowing he messed up, and allowing Gibbs to sugarcoat his stupidity would be a copout. "I should have listened to her. It isn't like she wasn't right about all the murders my father committed."

"Can you tell me about her dream?"

"Another death. A female. She didn't give me many details because she could tell I didn't believe it was a vision. And I didn't ask."

"Could it be Ava's death she saw in her premonition?"

Cole hadn't considered that. But then he dismissed it, saying, "I don't think so. She had the vision early this morning, and I saw Ava later in the coffee shop." A disturbing realization ricocheted across his mind. Jenna had a vision about her own death days ago. It hadn't come to pass...yet. Perhaps, the visions she was haunted with now were not happening in the same sequence of time as the ones she'd had about his father's murder victims. She could be seeing these visions days before they occur in real time. If that were the case, she could still be in danger of the premonition she'd had about being buried alive. At first, he'd questioned who would want to do that. The threat from his father had passed many months ago. But now, a new threat was on the horizon. Someone was planning something. "Listen," he told Gibbs, his heart in his throat, "I'm only a couple minutes away from my house. I'm going to see if Jenna is here. I've got to track her down. I don't think she's safe."

"Okay, man. Let me know if you need me. I'll stay vigilant."

****

Tears streamed down Jenna's face as she tottered down Cole's porch steps hauling heavy luggage in both hands. It was wishful thinking he would have stormed through the doors and interrupted her while she was packing. She would have taken one look at his face and crumbled, surrendering her bleeding heart to the will of his.

Pull yourself together. Being this weak wasn't in her nature, but then, where it concerned Cole, her normal attributes were thrown out the window. She just wanted things to go back to the way they were before their awful argument this morning, and before she'd discovered his ex-girlfriend kissed him. *And which way was that, exactly? It's not like he had faith in your visions prior to any of those things taking place.*

Why did she have to be so persistent when it came to him accepting her clairvoyant abilities? Because it was important, that's why. It was such a big part of her identity. And if he couldn't reconcile with that, then he didn't know her at all.

She popped the trunk and heaved the suitcases inside. But as she headed to the driver's side, she couldn't stem the flow of tears that kept coming. Being at odds with Cole and being without him was the most miserable feeling in the world.

She climbed in and dried her eyes for the twentieth

time today. She was a sniveling fool and she needed to get a grip.

Barbara called as she backed out of Cole's driveway. "Hello."

"How are you holding up?" her best friend asked, her voice a soft lull.

"I'd like to say great, but that's not the case."

"I just wish you'd take my advice and try to work things out with Cole. You two love each other and look how miserable you are."

"Do you think I haven't tried?"

"Maybe you haven't tried hard enough."

Jenna plucked another tissue from the box sitting in the passenger's seat and blotted her tears. That's how pathetic she was. A few tissues wouldn't do, so she'd had to stop at a gas station on the way here and purchase a whole box. "Nothing I say will make him feel any different. Besides, you can't stand him. I'd figured if anyone would be jumping for joy we weren't getting along, it would be you."

"That's not fair, Jenna."

She sighed, tossing the wadded tissue amongst the dozen others littering her passenger's seat. "I know. I'm sorry. I didn't mean it. I haven't been this upset since my mother dragged me away from Cole over ten years ago."

"Which is exactly why you need to talk to him, Jenna."

"I have."

"Talk to him again, then."

On top of everything, she wanted to tug her hair out now. "You're not helping, Barb."

"I'm not trying to make you feel worse, I'm just

trying to talk some sense into you. Did you make it there yet?"

"I'm on my way to your house now."

"Don't forget where I told you the key is."

"Under the fake rock next to the doormat, right? I wanted to thank you again for letting me stay at your house tonight."

"You can stay as long as you need. You know that. My door is always open for you. I'm just sorry I can't be there with you tonight. I know you could really use my company."

Jenna sniffled and veered onto the long stretch of road leading to Barb's house. "It's okay. You already made plans to help Dunston with his move to the house in Arlington. How's that going?"

"We got everything loaded into the moving truck. We've been on the road for awhile now. We're probably, oh, about ten minutes away from his house in Arlington. I'm waiting out in the truck at a gas station while Dunston ran in to get us something cold to drink."

"You two are getting along really well, huh?"

Barbara didn't say anything.

Jenna understood why. Barb didn't want to mention the highlights of her love life while her best friend was going through Hell with hers. "It's okay. You can talk about it. I'm so happy you found someone you enjoy spending time with. You deserve this."

"I'd be lying if I didn't say things are going great between us. He's such a giving person. Always showering me with the things he thinks will make me comfortable."

The same way Cole had done for her many times.

Jenna attempted a smile through the stab of pain in her heart. Things were finally looking up for Barbara. And it couldn't have happened to a better person. "Listen, I'm about to pull into your driveway."

"Okay. I'll let you get settled in. Call me if you have trouble finding anything. I should be home sometime tomorrow, and we'll talk then."

That was code word for, I'm going to drive you crazy until you see things my way, Jenna realized, her attention floating toward the heavens.

She shuffled out of the car, grabbing her purse, and then backtracked, plucking the box of tissues from the seat. With the way things were going, and how desperately she missed Cole, she'd need them again before the night was through.

.

Chapter Nine

Cole tore through his house until ending up in the bedroom. He headed straight for the closet, and fear gripped him the moment he realized Jenna's suitcases were missing. When he peered at the dresser, he noticed a few drawers slightly open, and the lacy strap of a bra hanging out. Dammit, what time had she arrived, and how long had she spent packing?

His tired legs carried him to the kitchen, where he sat down in the same chair she had planted herself in this morning, at the start of that dreadful argument which had dominated the entire day. He wished he had a rewind button. If he could have guessed the disagreement would cause her to ignore him and then pack up and leave, he'd have handled things so much differently.

But that was the bitch of not being mindful of your actions before you took them. Now, he was left with a belly of burning regret. The pieces of their life together were scattered all over the floor, and he'd have to figure out how to put them back in place again, and quickly, before any harm came to her.

Yet, as he sat there another moment, he had to ask himself, where was his faith in her? Then it dawned on him. It wasn't that he didn't believe she was having visions again, it was that he didn't want to believe it. The last time she had premonitions, awful things happened. They'd put those tragic events behind them. They were moving on together toward a life of happiness, and then fate stepped in with a different plan the day Jenna had another vision.

But it would always be this way with her, wouldn't it? The reality hadn't sunk in before. She had been given this gift, and it couldn't be shut off like a spigot just because he wanted to live a fairy tale life with her. Loving Jenna Langley and spending the rest of his days with her meant accepting who she was.

And she was a psychic for better or worse. It wasn't ever going to change.

He lowered his head, realizing what she'd been trying to show him. It wasn't enough he loved her with all his heart. She wanted him to accept her for who she was. She tried to open his eyes to this when they were teenagers, from the moment she had her first premonition. He didn't believe her then. And now...

What a blind fool he'd been. Now she was in danger. He needed to find her.

Where could she have gone?

He grabbed his phone to call her again. As it rang, he clung to the hope she'd pick up this time. It went to voicemail. This time he left a message begging her to get in touch with him, explaining all he'd discovered concerning Ava, and apologizing for being too blind to see what she'd been trying to show him. He ended the message by letting her know he was concerned for her safety, and to please call him back immediately.

But as he swiped his finger across the phone, ending the call, an idea occurred to him, and he wondered why he hadn't considered it earlier. Probably too busy running Ava down. Although he may not know where Jenna went, he'd bet Barbara did.

After placing the call, Barbara finally answered on the fifth ring. "What do you want, asshole?"

"Hello to you, too."

"I wasn't going to waste a greeting on you."

"Did I do something to you today?"

"You did something to my best friend. It's the same thing, pal."

"I know. But that's not why I'm calling."

"So, you admit it?"

"What, am I on trial here?"

"You're sure as hell in the doghouse. I can tell you that."

Rightly noted. "Jenna packed up and left my house. Do you know where she went?"

"As if I'd tell you," she said, her voice raising an octave.

"I think she's in danger. You need to tell me where she went, Barbara."

"In danger of what?"

"I don't have time to go into it. Where is she?"

"You know, you could have prevented this whole thing by just telling Jenna that woman kissed you."

"That's none of your business." The nerve of this woman never ceased to amaze him.

"Oh, trust me, Jenna has made it my business. She's been on the phone with me all day crying over it. I don't understand why you didn't just tell her the truth."

"Because I didn't want to upset her."

"That worked out really well, didn't it?"

Anger coiled in the pit of Cole's stomach. "I don't have to explain anything to you. Just tell me where she is."

"What makes you think I know?"

"Because she tells you everything."

"And that just crawls all over you, doesn't it?"

"Barbara!"

"What?"

"This isn't some pissing contest. If I don't find her, something terrible can happen to her. Do you want that on your conscience?"

"Exactly what's going on here?"

He closed his eyes against the irritation that wound through him. He wasn't getting anywhere until he tossed her a bone. "Fine. I found out Ava quite her job and moved out of her house. Some guy hired a PI on her behalf to snap pictures of me and Ava at the venue. Something's going on that involves me and Jenna, but I haven't quite figured out what yet. All of that coupled with Jenna's visions makes me fear the worst for her."

"I told her not to trust that woman. I knew from the beginning she didn't have good intentions. Why in the world did you agree to let her hire Ava in the first place?"

"It's not like I've ever been able to stop her from doing anything, and I have a feeling it wouldn't have mattered anyhow. From all the evidence I've been collecting, Ava and her accomplice hatched this plan from the beginning. She would have seen it through one way or the other."

"So, what are you going to do about it?"

"Get her location from you for starters. So I can protect her."

"She's at my house. She called earlier and asked if she could stay there tonight."

"Are you with her?"

"I'm in Arlington helping Dunston move into his house. I'm not coming back until tomorrow. So, you're going after her, right?'

"I'm going to pop a bag of popcorn and start watching season one of Vampire's Lair. That's what I'm going to do."

"Smartass."

"Back at ya."

"Just hurry, okay. I didn't take her seriously when she told me about her vision of being buried alive. And now I'm worried about her."

He could kick himself in the ass for the same thing. Hopefully, it wasn't too late to rectify that. He headed toward the door, snatching his truck keys out of his pocket, and saying, "I'm leaving now."

"Call me and let me know when you get to her, please."

He slipped his phone into his pocket and hopped into his truck. Apprehension swallowed him whole as he started the engine and tore out of the driveway. He prayed to God he could get to her before the sinking premonition in the pit of his gut became a reality.

****

Jenna sat at the kitchen table in her robe, fresh from a shower, hair wrapped in a towel, and debating whether she should listen to his voice message. The phone was in her hand when Cole's call came in. She let it ring several times, and a few minutes after it stopped, the distinctive ringtone alerted her she had a new voicemail.

He'd called and texted a few times throughout the day. But he had yet to leave a message.

Jenna munched on her bottom lip. Maybe it was important, and that's why he left a voicemail. Or perhaps he was using a new tactic to get her to call him back. What if he'd heard from their daughter Emily and something was wrong?

Emily was fine, and most likely enjoying her trip at Disneyland with her grandparents. Besides, if their daughter needed to get in touch with them, she'd call Jenna's phone. She always had.

She didn't need to hear Cole's voice right now. It would only bring on the heartache she'd been doing her best to forget ever since she arrived at Barb's house. The shower was a good start. It helped to relax and refresh her, even though she had a suspicion it would be short-lived.

Mind made up, she laid the phone on the table and strolled into the bedroom, opening her suitcase, and rummaging through it for something comfortable to wear. She found a pair of loose-fitting jeans, a tee-shirt, and sandals. They'd work just fine.

But after changing into the clothes and slipping back into the kitchen for a cold drink, her attention wandered to the table where her phone sat. Why did he leave a message this time? Before she had thirty more seconds to ponder that again, her phone alerted her she had a missed call. She stepped over to the table and stared down at the device. Had Cole tried to call her while she'd been changing? She hadn't heard the phone go off. But the bedroom was far enough away from the kitchen she probably wouldn't have heard it. She took a deep breath and then snatched up the device, checking the missed call. It was Barbara.

She clicked on the number to redial. It rang several

times with no response. Then, without taking a minute to think about it, she punched in her password to check her messages. Cole's husky voice boomed in her ears, shaking her to her core.

"I'm so sorry, honey. I'd give anything to take back how I acted. And I get it. I see what you were trying to show me. To be honest, it wasn't that I didn't believe you were having visions, I think more than anything I was afraid you were. That fear drove me to deny it was happening again. But it's not your fault. This is a gift God saw fit to give you, for whatever reason he did. I have come to realize it is a part of who you are. And I love you, Jenna Langley. Visions and all. If you'll give me another chance, I promise to show you I can be a better partner.

This is much deeper than I originally thought, and I really need you to call me back. I found out Ava moved out of her house and quit her job. Some guy, using a stolen credit card paid the PI to take those pictures of me and Ava. These two are planning something, and I think you and I are the target. Please, honey, you need to come back home immediately. Oh, God, Jenna. Call me."

Alarm bells blasted through Jenna's head at the concern in his voice. The vision she had days ago about being buried alive caused her breath to catch in her chest. It was foolish to have believed any premonition had been the product of a symbolic dream. No matter what Professor Delaney said, in her soul she'd known better all along. What could Ava and this unknown man have to gain by causing her and Cole harm? Although she realized Ava and Cole had a romantic history, now that she and Cole were about to marry, to take things this far was insane.

Moved out of her house and quit her job? Where did she go, and why did she leave so quickly? And who was this unknown guy Cole mentioned, and why did he hire a private investigator to take pictures of Cole and his ex-lover?

She feared Cole was right, and they were both at the center of some twisted plot to cause them harm. With her heart near to beating out of her chest, she gathered her purse, car keys, and phone, and headed toward the front door of Barbara's house. With each step, her breathing became harsher.

Once outside, her hands trembled as she fought to snap open the fake rock and retrieve the house key.

The key slipped out of her hand and hit the cement stoop with a loud *ting*. The sound shot through her like a bolt of lightning. She plunked it off the ground, and crammed it into the keyhole, twisting it with such force it was a wonder the thing didn't break off inside the lock.

The sensation she needed to get the hell out of here now grew by leaps and bounds as she worked to stuff the key back into the fake stone. The hairs on the nape of her neck stood on end, and she ran for her car. Awareness of something dark and sinister approaching awakened her sixth sense.

The closer she got to her vehicle, the more sluggish her steps became. *Oh God, please no. Not now.* Horror settled over her as she collapsed to the ground. She was within an arm's length of her car, but she was so weakened by the oncoming vision she couldn't muster the strength to reach for the handle.

She should have called Cole the second she'd

finished listening to his voicemail. Then he would have known where she was and could have come to rescue her. Instead, she now lay shriveled up on the ground, all alone and completely helpless to the horrible fate coming for her.

Close to paralyzed, she stared into the endless abyss of a sky as it shifted into darkness. Patterns, each a different color, swirled before her eyes, then faded out. An image appeared of a red car pulling into a driveway. The vision was so vivid, the car's exhaust pipe rattled as it rolled to a stop. The driver's side door swung open, and a tall, slender blonde stepped out. The stranger spun and stared directly at her. Jenna's heart pounded when she recognized her face.

What was she doing? And was it Barbara's house she'd driven up to?

"My my my. Look at you," Ava Kingsley sneered, standing over someone on the ground and peering down at them. Her face twisted into a sarcastic imitation of sympathy. "Are you having one of those visions again?" She clucked her tongue, shaking her head. "I heard about those. But I wasn't sure if they were real. That must be hell. No way to live if you ask me."

Jenna realized without a doubt the person Ava was talking to was her. Had she been in the middle of a vision, or was this really happening?

"I'm going to kidnap you now. You can either get up and walk to my car, or I can drag you by the hair of your head. Your choice."

My God, it had to be real, Jenna realized as a drop of sweat rolled down Ava's face. None of her previous visions had been clear enough that she'd ever witnessed someone perspiring. The woman swiped the fluid away, saying, "Oh dear. You can't move, can you?"

Jenna struggled to open her mouth, twitch an eye, anything. Just as with all the other times when her visons had taken over, nothing ever worked. She was defenseless and would remain so until this immobile state came to pass.

"That's okay," Ava said, moving around to her head. The crunching of limestone under the woman's feet as she shuffled about made what was happening to her all too real. It couldn't be a vision. But if it weren't, why couldn't she move?

"We'll improvise. Even if it's a big, fat waste of my time."

Something tugged on Jenna's hair, and sharp rocks dug into her flesh as her body slid across the driveway. "I guess you want to know why I'm doing this," Ava said, lugging her along. "I can admit, I was a little sore when your fiancé broke it off with me a year ago. But it wasn't the end of the world. A girl like me has endless opportunities. I never needed Cole Rainwater to better my life anyhow. Although, he was a bitch to get over. You can relate, huh?" she said, peering down at Jenna, as she finally came to rest at the rear of Ava's car. "C'mon, honey, let's get you into the trunk."

Jenna's body lifted off the ground as Ava grunted and heaved. When she was finally settled into the trunk, the woman continued talking. "Now, where was I? Oh, yes. Cole's charming little ways. If I'm being honest, I guess there's still a part of me that would love to jump his bones one last time. But it doesn't look like that's going to happen. He's not very happy with me since I put sugar in your gas tank." She snorted. "He'd be downright pissed if he found out I kidnapped his precious little psychic. But it doesn't matter. I'll be long gone by then."

She grabbed a white cloth out of her pocket and wiped the sweat from her face. "I'm afraid my motive isn't very romantic. I'm doing it for the money. And your fiancé has come into quite a bit of it. I figure he owes me after all he's put me through. So, I'm going to turn you over to my business partner, and he's going to ransom you off." Ava winked, the expression on her face as pleased as if she'd hit the lottery. "Don't you worry your pretty, little head none though, honey. I'm sure Cole will pay a king's fortune to get you back. He's pathetic that way."

She put her hand on the top of the trunk as if to shut Jenna in, then thought better of it. She chuckled. "Oh, I almost forgot." She whipped out a gun from the back of her waist. "Even though I didn't need my little Luger to convince you to come with me, compliments of your visions, it looks like I'll need it to knock you out. Can't have you snapping back to your senses when this clairvoyant episode of yours is all over."

The butt of the gun crashed down on her head, and the world floated into darkness.

****

The instant Cole pulled into Barb's driveway, he saw Jenna's purse lying open on the asphalt behind her car. The driver's side door stood open; Cole couldn't get out of his truck fast enough.

Oh, God, no. He spotted her phone a good two feet from her purse. Small rocks were scattered about, as if someone dragged something huge across the driveway leading to the spot where his truck now sat. A large object, like a body. Even though Cole stood there in shock, his detective instincts kicked in.

The spilled purse, the phone laying at a distance, and the drag marks indicated whatever took place happened right here. Jenna was in this spot when she was besieged by someone. She'd packed her suitcases when she left his house. But there wasn't any luggage out here with her purse and phone. Something caused her to make a hasty exit from Barb's house.

Could she have gotten rattled when she heard his message warning her he was concerned she may not be safe due to his suspicious discoveries regarding Ava and this unknown co-conspirator? Or could someone have either shown up at Barbara's house, or called her phone threatening her?

He headed toward the house to investigate whether there were signs of a struggle inside but paused at the last moment remembering her car door was left open. Perhaps, he ought to check inside the car first for any evidence she may have left behind as to her whereabouts.

The first thing he noticed when he peered inside, was an envelope lying neatly on the driver's side seat, as if it had been put there after the probable kidnapping of his fiancée had taken place. He handled the envelope carefully, not wanting to destroy the possibility of lifting fingerprints from it and sliced open the top with his pocketknife. He drew out a typed letter addressed to him.

A whoosh of air expelled from his lungs the instant he read what they'd done with Jenna. She was buried in a grave six feet under, with only a breathing hose and a battery-operated fan pumping oxygen into a casket. After twenty hours, the oxygen would cut off, and she would suffocate. The vision she had had about being buried alive crashed through his mind. Everyone tried to convince her it was only a symbolic dream, but it had been a premonition of the horror to come. And he'd realized it too late.

The kidnappers demanded a ransom of one-hundred million dollars. And they were giving him two hours to drop off the cash to an address they provided. The note went on to explain if he pulled any funny business, got the authorities involved, or if the police staked out the drop off location, the precious air keeping Jenna alive would be cut off sooner. Once he dropped off the money, and the kidnappers had it in hand, he would be given Jenna's location.

Now it made perfect sense. Ava Kingsley wasn't running from something. She had been preparing to pull off a major kidnapping for ransom, and she had someone helping her do it. Something this huge could not be carried off alone. But how in the world could she have known he had access to that kind of money? With enough digging, she could have uncovered that information. Just the way she discovered he and Jenna hadn't hired a wedding planner. Cole had to wonder how long Ava had been in the shadows planning to kidnap his fiancée and ransom her off for his inheritance. Had she been keeping tabs on him since he ended the relationship with her a year ago? Had she planned her revenge once she discovered the details of what his great-grandfather left for him? A shiver ran up his spine at the consideration she may have been following them around and spying on them for God knows how long.

He snatched out his phone and dialed Gibbs'

number.

"Hey, man. What's up?" his partner asked.

Cole took a deep breath, doing his best to stay calm, and said, "I'm at Barbara Cassidy's house where Jenna has been staying. I just arrived a few minutes ago, and I found her purse and phone lying in the driveway. Her car door was left open along with a ransom note on the seat. They've kidnapped her, Gibbs. I can't believe it."

"Jesus. Any idea where they would have taken her?"

He was a hairsbreadth away from losing it and allowing the panic that was threatening to set in to take full reign over his emotions. He had been through rigorous police training. Giving in to anxiety in a critical situation like this was the wrong thing to do. But it was Jenna's life on the line. If he couldn't find her in twenty hours, she'd suffocate in a small box all alone.

"The letter claims they have her buried underground somewhere. There's enough oxygen to keep her alive for the next twenty hours. I'm supposed to bring one-hundred million dollars in cash to a drop off location. Then they'll give me her location."

"Did they say how they plan to get this information to you?"

"Not yet."

Gibbs exhaled loudly, and the realization of what his partner was about to say twisted in Cole's gut. He spoke up before his buddy could. "I realize the chance they'll tell me where she is once I release the money is slim to none. I've been in law enforcement long enough to know how this kind of shit usually goes down. But this is my fiancée we're talking about here. If there's a chance—"

"There isn't. They won't risk getting caught by contacting you like that. They'll take the money and run."

Cole lowered his head. Even though it wasn't what he wanted to hear, and he'd give every single possession he owned on this earth to get Jenna back, he couldn't deny the truth of his partner's words. All they wanted was the money and they'd be gone. The only way to save her would be to track them down before twenty hours expired.

"Listen," Gibbs said, "I'm going to contact a friend of mine, Dylan Cruz. He's a Texas Ranger and works for the Special Response Teams. He's handled this type of thing before, and I know he'll be a big help."

Cole shook his head, dead set against Gibbs' idea. "You know the risk of getting another agency involved. Things can get messy in a heartbeat. If they show up at the drop off location, no matter how covert they think they're being, there's a chance the kidnappers will know. If that happens, they're threatening to cut off her oxygen earlier. I can't risk that."

"This department has never handled anything like this. We don't have the experience to deal with this. But he does. Will you trust me on this?"

"I don't think it's a good idea. We need to handle this ourselves."

"Do you remember the kidnapping of Evelyn Harper, two years ago?"

Cole recalled the face of the woman. A beautiful young nurse at a Dallas hospital. She had been kidnapped and held for ransom by an aggrieved ex-employee of her millionaire father who owned several lucrative check cashing businesses across the United States. The poor girl had been held hostage for three horrifying days. She had been found in a condemned, abandoned house in east Texas, tied to a bed, flea ridden, and dehydrated. The fact the father paid the ransom was not what saved his daughter's life. The kidnapper never gave up her location. They finally found the bastard staying in a motel close to the border of Mexico, where he had planned to make his escape. As for the victim, her whereabouts were discovered through damn good investigative work.

"Yeah," Gibbs finally said. "It was Cruz who found that girl when no one else could."

Although Cole remembered The Texas Rangers had been involved in her rescue, he wasn't sure who the agent was who was responsible for bringing Evelyn home. Perhaps, Gibbs was right, and they could use this guy's help. "Okay, make the call. But news of this cannot get out to anyone else. The last thing we need to do is tip off the kidnappers another agency is involved."

"You got it. I'm going to have Channing put out an APB on Ava Kingsley's car. We may not know who else is involved in this, but if we find Ava, we have a helluva lot better chance of acquiring that information. I'm about to head your way, and I'm bringing a few of the guys with me. What's the address?"

As Cole rambled off the address to Barb's house, the fear they may not make it in time to rescue Jenna squeezed his heart with a renewed sense of desperation. He couldn't think like that. It was his lack of faith in her visions to begin with that allowed this horror to be brought to her doorstep. If he'd have trusted her when

183

she warned him this was coming, he would have been more vigilant much sooner on. He could have prevented this if he had paid attention to the signs.

And what signs were those? It wasn't as if he ever could have guessed a kiss from what he thought to be a jealous ex-girlfriend would lead to the kidnapping and deadly threat against his fiancée. It didn't matter. If he hadn't questioned her visions, and told her about the kiss when it happened, they never would have been at odds with one another, and it wouldn't have been so easy for Ava to have come between them, causing them to stay away from each other long enough for her to get to Jenna. Was it his ex-girlfriend who did the kidnapping, her co-partner in crime, or both? And where in the hell did they take her?

Instead of going out of his mind with helpless worry while he waited for Gibbs and the guys to get here, he decided to investigate the inside of the house to see if there were any clues left behind by Jenna or her kidnappers. The best thing he could do was keep busy and continue working to solve this mystery. Giving into the urge to completely fall apart wouldn't do anyone any good, least of all Jenna who needed him to be strong and rely on his instincts to figure out where they'd taken her.

He grabbed the doorknob and found it locked, further cementing his belief the attack took place outside in the driveway. If the assailants, or assailant, had encountered Jenna inside, they wouldn't have bothered to lock the door on their way out. It would have been Jenna who locked the door, and he'd wager, soon after she did, her attackers showed up.

Chapter Ten

At the same time a sharp intake of breath filled her lungs, Jenna's eyes snapped open. Blackness surrounded her; panic set in instantly as soft whimpers set off a series of echoes. It took a moment for it to sink in the sounds were her own.

Raising both hands, her palms struck a hard object not a foot above her head. She slid her palms over a rough surface, searching, feeling across the top and down the sides of what felt like a wooden crate.

That embodied her like a tomb.

She let go a shriek, crying out in agony, "No! no! please, no!" There was no doubt she was in the very place that stoked the deepest fear in her heart. Just the way her vision forewarned. She was buried alive.

Loud beeping filled the tiny space. As soon as it dissipated, a light snapped on at the foot of the casket and infrared digits blinked to life on the ceiling, directly above her face. Nineteen hours, and thirty-one minutes flashed in succession, like the clock of doom counting down the final hours and minutes of her life.

She distinctly recalled her vision. The clock counting down from two hours. And it occurred to her if her premonition was accurate, it meant she was going to be in here for a long time.

God, no!

Renewed terror besieged her like a wildfire

ravaging trees and decaying brush as it swept across a forest floor. She couldn't imagine being trapped in here that long. In her vision she remembered hearing a fan softly humming somewhere inside. She stilled, listening for the sound. It was a faint buzz, but apparent, nonetheless. If there was a fan, perhaps, there would also be a breathing hose. Although the light at the foot of the casket was small and dim, when she peered around, twisting her head to study the board behind her, it allowed enough of a visual to spot the small fan affixed into the wall of the casket. She breathed a sigh of relief. She'd have enough air, she imagined, until the clock above her head reached zero. What did it matter anyhow? It's not like anyone would find her here, buried God knows how many feet under the ground.

Ava's words floated back to her. *Don't you worry your pretty, little head none though, honey. I'm sure Cole will pay a king's fortune to get you back.*

She was being held for ransom. Cole would have been contacted by now. Surely he'd make it in time to save her. All Ava and her partner wanted was a payoff. They weren't looking to commit murder, right? But she'd seen enough movies to know these kidnapping for ransom schemes rarely went as planned. What if something went terribly wrong and Cole could not get to her in time, or at all? She could lie dead in this grave for the next twenty years and no one would ever know.

That was impossible. If there was a fan, there would have to be a ventilating hose above ground. It would be visible and possibly alert a passerby to some nefarious goings on. But of course, the kidnappers would not have placed her in a location that was easy for anyone to spot. They would have dug this grave somewhere out of the way. No one would find her anytime soon. It would have defeated their purpose to do anything else.

To make matters worse, the clock in her vision counted down two hours. That wasn't a lot of time for Cole to find her or someone else to discover this grave. Why didn't she listen to him when he warned her at the office Ava was up to no good? She ignored his calls and texts all day and ran around like a fool immersed in her own woe-is-me party. She should have been alert. She had the nerve to accuse him of not taking her visions seriously, when she, herself didn't heed her own premonitions. She had been angry at him for not trusting her, but she hadn't trusted him at all, had she?

All the regret and wishful thinking in the world would not get her out of this. And she couldn't very well claw her way to the surface.

The first wave of sobs racked her body. Grief and anxiety surged through her like the swelling of the ocean tide rolling against the shore. How stupid could a person be? It wasn't as if she wasn't forewarned about this omen through clairvoyance. But she'd allowed others to convince her it was nothing more than a symbolic dream. It had been a sick joke at her expense, and probably the last one she'd ever experience.

As she lay there in a tiny casket, drowning in her misery, and fighting furiously to overcome the raw fear threatening to send her into the throes of blind madness, the light at the foot of the casket switched off, and the digital clock went black, plunging her into total darkness again. Her guttural wails reverberated off the walls of the small enclosure, reminding her of a death cry.

****

After searching the house and finding nothing, Cole went outside just in time to see two patrol units converging on the house. Gibbs and an unfamiliar man stepped out of the car parked closest. As they approached, Cole got a better view of the lean figure of the guy. The brown uniform and cowboy hat, along with the official Texas Ranger badge pinned above the fellow's left shirt pocket gave him all the introduction he would have needed.

"Cole, this is Agent Dylan Cruz," Gibbs said. "Texas Ranger for the Special Response Teams I told you about over the phone."

The man with the dark hair and striking blue eyes stuck his hand out. Cole shook it, noticing right away the strong grip of the guy. "At your service, Detective Rainwater. I wish we could be meeting under better circumstances."

Cole lowered his head and nodded.

"I just want you to know my team and I will do everything in our power to find out where they took your fiancée," Cruz promised.

When Cole stared into the man's eyes, it was undeniable he meant business.

Channing and Prebis strolled over to Cole and clapped him on the back. Channing said, "We're going to find these bastards and bring Jenna home."

Every hope Cole dared to cling to wanted to believe they would. Any other outcome was simply unacceptable.

Cruz asked, "Can I see the ransom note?"

Cole strode over to Jenna's car where he'd left the letter sitting and grabbed it out of the driver's seat.

Before handing it to the Texas Ranger, he warned him to be careful as he'd want to check it as evidence for fingerprints.

Cruz removed the letter from the envelope, passing it to Gibbs, and cautiously unfolded the paper to read for himself. After a few minutes, Cruz said, "She may have longer than twenty hours."

"I don't understand," Cole admitted.

"The average person has a little more than one hundred liters of oxygen in their body," Cruz explained. "If they used up half a liter every minute, it would roughly take about five to five and a half hours to consume all their oxygen. This is not set in stone, though. There are many factors inside the casket that could alter her breathing conditions. I was also briefed Jenna has psychic abilities. Did she happen to see any of this in a vision?"

Cole found it odd the man would ask that. "About a week ago, she woke from a vision and told me she saw herself in a casket. She mentioned a time clock counting down from two hours. She said she could hear a fan humming. She had the feeling once the clock reached zero, the fan would stop working."

"The note from the kidnappers states the time clock would be set for twenty hours," Cruz mentioned. "But in her vision, she saw it counting down from two hours?"

"That's what has me worried," Cole admitted. "I don't know if it will take us that long to find her, or if the kidnappers were lying about the time she has."

"Did she see anything outside the casket? Anything that might give us a clue as to where she is?"

Cole shook his head. "That's what's been so

frustrating. When she has a vision, she's never seen anything outside the area of what's taking place."

"What about other visions? Has she had additional ones recently?"

He frowned, considering the premonition she had early this morning. But he didn't see how the two could be connected. "She witnessed a man killing a woman this morning. But the house was dark, and she couldn't see any faces."

Cruz's expression was set in deep thought. "A dark house."

"You don't think the two are connected?" Cole asked.

"I'd bet they are," the agent answered.

Cole found it odd the guy took such an interest in Jenna's visions. Most people working in law enforcement didn't believe in clairvoyance—or those who claimed to have it. Lord knows he'd struggled with it himself. "Do you believe in premonitions, Agent Cruz?"

The man frowned, as if he were more insightful about this subject than Cole had given him credit for. "I've worked with many people just like Jenna. My sister-in-law is psychic. So, yes, detective, I believe there are people in this universe who have the ability to see what most of us can't."

He could probably take some pointers from this guy. At the least, he should have embraced this attitude where it concerned Jenna long ago.

Cruz said, "If it's a dark house it's either abandoned, or the electricity has been cut off for some reason. Could be a house someone has moved out of or is moving into."

What the agent said reminded him of the conditions he'd found in Ava's house. "I checked Ava Kingsley's house earlier today. Everything is moved out. No water or electricity."

The agent's brows furrowed. He asked for the address and Cole gave it to him. Next, Cruz got on the radio clipped to his right shoulder and gave instructions to his team to send a few men over to stake out the house.

For the first time Cole took notice of dusk on the horizon. In another thirty minutes, the sun would have completely gone down. Could Jenna's vision have taken place inside Ava's house? Is that where a murder would occur? Who could be the victim? Ava? Someone else? He no longer questioned whether Cruz was on his game. He'd taken notice of a clue right out in the open Cole hadn't even thought to consider. A little more hope was restored in his soul. Gibbs had been right. Bringing the agent on was a smart move.

"Any sign of a struggle inside?" Gibbs asked.

"Nope. I checked. I could tell Jenna took a shower recently. And she locked the door behind her. So, whoever attacked her did it after she stepped off the stoop."

Just then, the crackle of Gibbs' radio startled all of them. *"Gibbs, this is Browning. You read?"*

Cole recognized the name as from one of the officers, a rookie, who worked the night shift at the Farmersville PD.

Gibbs clicked the talk button on his radio and answered the guy. "Go ahead."

"We just got a hit on Ava Kingsley's car. It was seen leaving the Motel Seven about two hours ago."

"What do you mean two hours ago?" Gibbs growled. The expression on his face told Cole he wondered why anyone would wait two hours to report the sighting. "Who called it in?"

"Some kid who works the front desk over there. He has a police scanner and was listening in during his break. He heard the description of the car and the driver, and realized he'd recognized both pulling up in front of the hotel yesterday. He'd waited on the woman who rented a room. About two hours ago, she came down to the lobby and checked out."

Cole realized Ava must have checked out of the motel before the attack on Jenna. He had difficulty believing a small woman like Ava could handle Jenna on her own. Did her partner take care of that detail while she headed off somewhere else?

Cruz motioned toward Gibbs' radio as if asking permission to talk to Browning. "This is agent Dylan Cruz, Texas Ranger with the Special Response Teams. I'm working with detectives here to track down Jenna Langley. I need you to head over to the motel. Get on the phone with the witness and find out all the information you can about his dealings with the suspect. Tell them to pull the footage from the cameras outside the parking lot, inside the lobby, and in the hallway leading to the room Ms. Kingsley was staying in. I'll need to know if anyone spotted her with someone else, what name she used to rent the room, and what method was used to pay for it. Find out if her room has been cleaned yet, and if so, what they did with the trash that came out of it. Then report back to us, okay?"

"Yes, sir. I'll get on that right now."

Cruz threw a glance in Cole's direction as he headed toward the cruiser. "Would you like to ride with us, detective?"

"Damn right I would."

****

Browning stood outside the Motel Seven, waiting for them as they drove up to the covered area in front of the establishment. "They've pulled the video footage Agent Cruz asked for," the kid told him. "It's sitting in the surveillance room inside the motel waiting to be viewed."

"What about the statement of the motel worker who interacted with Ava Kingsley?" Cruz asked from the driver's seat.

Browning checked his notebook. "He saw her drive up at the front of the motel around seven p.m. yesterday. She left her car sitting here while she rented the room. He reported there was no one in the car with her, and as you can see—" He pointed straight toward the double-glass doors leading into the atrium of the motel. "—there's a decent view from here into the lobby. The front desk is right there. The desk clerk said he could clearly see her drive up and get out of the car and she was alone in the vehicle. I've also talked to a few other workers who were here last night. None of them saw anyone with her, including the bell hop who delivered dinner to her room."

Cruz nodded at the kid. "I appreciate you coming out here and checking on things."

The officer's eyes lit up. Cole recognized the thrill oozing from the kid's expression like glaze dripping from a fresh-baked pastry. He'd carried that same sense of untamed adventure once. It came at that point when you realize writing traffic tickets and handling domestic disputes no longer fed the need for more. The rookie wanted to be in the action, playing on the court with the big boys.

After years of working in the homicide unit, if Cole could tell him anything, he'd warn him it's not all it's cracked up to be. Better save yourself the heartache that comes with knocking on someone's door to inform them their loved one has met their demise at the hands of the worst of the worst. The dark side of humanity was what nightmares were made of. And once you've walked in their world and witnessed the crimes they commit, there was no escaping back to a normal life ever again. But he had a feeling his words would have fallen on deaf ears.

They cruised around to a parking spot and got out. Channing met him halfway to the lobby doors and handed him his truck keys. Cole thanked him for driving it here, giving him a chance to brief Cruz on his earlier findings in the case while on the way.

After they checked with the front desk to inquire about whether the trash had already been removed from Ava's room, and were told, indeed it had, and a few of the janitors were searching for it now, he, Cruz, and Gibbs headed toward the surveillance room.

A man dressed in a blue-collar shirt and black slacks sitting at a computer desk glanced their way as they entered the room. He was an attractive guy, with slicked back, chestnut hair, and a trimmed goatee. The badge pinned to his shirt above the right pocket told Cole he was the motel security detail.

Cole nodded a greeting as the man rose from his chair.

Cruz spoke first. "I'm agent Cruz from The Texas Rangers, and these are Detectives Gibbs and Rainwater from the Farmersville PD."

The guard stuck out his hand, saying, "Daniel Lightfoot."

After everyone took turns shaking hands, Cole needed to move things along. "You were briefed on the video footage we requested, right?"

Lightfoot reclaimed his seat in front of the computer. "I have it right here. Which area do you want to view first?" he asked, busily moving his fingers over the keyboard.

Cole glanced at Cruz, and it was as if he could read his mind. "Let's start with the outside camera. I want to see if anyone accompanied the suspect here."

The security guard asked what timeframe they were interested in viewing, and Cole requested he cue up seven p.m., going with the time Browning informed them the desk clerk saw Ava drive up outside the motel. As they studied the recording, the timeclock on the camera ticked off the minutes. Nothing out of the ordinary jumped out at Cole. Then at about the ten-minute mark, an apple-red sports car pulled up under the pavilion. Cruz had Daniel slow down the footage.

In slow motion they watched Ava Kingsley step from the driver's side of the vehicle. With her purse strapped over her shoulder, and what appeared to be a set of car keys dangling from her right hand, she thrust open the double doors of the lobby, disappearing from the camera's view.

"Go ahead and speed it up," Cole told Daniel. When he did, a few more vehicles rolled through the parking lot, one backed out of a parking space and headed toward what he assumed was the road in front of the establishment, while another driver swung into the now vacant space and parked. Cole's attention drifted toward the timeclock. He noticed within ten minutes Ava made a second appearance. She headed to her car, settled in behind the wheel, and drove it the rest of the way around the circle-drive. Once the car took a left turn, heading toward the west end of the motel, it coasted out of sight.

Another few minutes ticked by, and just when Cole was about to suggest they switch to the camera overlooking the hallway to her room, she appeared again. This time she ambled toward the lobby doors with a duffel bag in one hand, and a manilla envelope in the other. "Pause the footage," Cole said, his eyes narrowing on the package in her hand.

Cruz pointed at the envelope. "What is that?"

"I don't know," Cole answered, "but we sure as hell need to find out."

The door creaked open, and every head spun toward the noise.

Channing poked his head in and said, "We've located the trash from Ava's room, and there's something here I think you should see."

Channing handed him a large, manilla envelope folded in half. He glanced back at the video footage and eyed the package in Ms. Kingsley's hand. Excitement rippled through him when he stared down at the one he now held. Could this be their first big break?

He didn't waste another minute as he carried the envelope over to a table, flipping it upside down, and sliding whatever contents were inside, out into the open.

He swore he'd been hit by a freight train the minute his brain registered he was staring at his uncle's dog tags, along with a small, white envelope.

As Cruz wandered over and picked up the envelope, Cole snatched up the dog tags. The name, *Rainwater, Derek,* was clearly stamped into the metal. A mental picture of his brother sitting at the attorney's office, opening the manilla envelope Jim Carter had handed him crashed through his mind. There existed only one way Ava Kingsley could get her hands on those dog tags.

Dunston Rainwater gave them to her.

When he glimpsed into Cruz's eyes, his own burning with sheer astonishment, he noticed confusion in their blue depths. The agent held up the small envelope in one hand, the figure, *five hundred thousand* scrawled across the front, and the slip of paper he'd obviously plucked from inside it in the other.

Cole snatched the paper—rage boiling inside him—and read the small, cursive writing. *You'll get the rest when you deliver Jenna Langley to me.*

Jesus Christ! His brother put Ava up to this. The woman didn't have a co-conspirator as he'd assumed. She was the co-conspirator. And his brother was the mastermind.

"This is the work of my brother, Dunston," Cole told Cruz, who stared at him as if he'd lost his mind.

"How do you know?" Cruz asked.

"Because he had possession of those dog tags, which belonged to my deceased uncle. He's paying Ava off to kidnap Jenna. We recently inherited some property and a shitload of money from our great grandfather. I received more than him. But I sold the business Hershel left me and offered to split the money with my brother. He acted like I offended him. It would have been more than enough money for him to retire for the rest of his life. So, it doesn't make sense for him to go to this extreme to collect more. I can't wrap my head around his motive."

"Then this isn't about money," Cruz said. "Does he have a grudge against you for some reason?"

Cole couldn't come up with a single reason why Dunston would have an axe to grind with him. "We met each other for the first time last week. I didn't even know he existed until the attorney handling my great-grandfather's will informed me."

"Did Dunston know about you?"

"If he did, he never mentioned it."

"Where is your brother?" Gibbs asked.

"At his house in Arlington." With that, the conversation he'd had earlier with Barbara clicked in his mind. She said she was with Dunston in Arlington helping him move into the house.

He picked up his phone and dialed her number. It rang several times, then went to voicemail. He cursed under his breath, and then dialed his brother's number. It didn't even ring before a voice recording came on. Either his phone was dead, or he'd purposely turned it off.

"Who are you calling?" Cruz stood there with a questioning stare.

"I talked to Jenna's best friend, Barbara, earlier today. She and Dunston are dating, and she mentioned to me she was with him, helping him move into his house in Arlington. Neither one of them are answering their phones."

Cole couldn't shake the disturbing scenarios that raced through his head. What if Dunston harmed Barbara? If she figured out his part in kidnapping Jenna, she'd be in grave danger.

"Is the electricity turned off in this house your brother is moving into?"

The expression on the agent's face struck a frantic chord in the pit of Cole's stomach. Jenna's vision ran rampant through his brain. A woman being murdered in a dark house. The house in her premonition had been one of three things: an abandoned dwelling, a place someone was moving into or moving out of.

Back at Barb's house, the agent had sent some of his team to stake out the place Ava deserted, believing that may have been the one in Jenna's vision. But it wasn't. It had been the house his brother inherited all along. It had to be. It would make sense the electricity wouldn't be turned on until his brother managed to switch the account over to his name. Could Barbara be the murdered woman in Jenna's vision?

"It'll take us over an hour to make it to Arlington from here," Cole said, thinking ahead, "that's if traffic isn't a bitch."

Cruz punched a number into his phone and placed it against his ear.

"Who are you calling?" Gibbs asked.

"A buddy of mine who owns a helicopter. Getting the Arlington PD involved will only slow down the investigation. We don't have time for that shit."

Cole frowned, shaking his head. One thing was glaringly obvious about Dylan Cruz. The guy did not screw around.

****

The chopper landed in a barren field only a few miles outside of Dunston's house in Arlington. The pilot killed the engine and as they filed out, Cole spotted the black SUV Cruz assured them would be waiting there. The agent knew a lot of people and was handy at calling in favors when he needed them.

When they were a few yards away from the vehicle, someone stepped from the driver's side. A tall, muscular man stood by the door waving at Cruz who waved back. Upon approaching, the guy grinned and embraced the agent in a man hug. "You never could stay out of trouble."

"Why would I when trouble is so entertaining?" Cruz's attention fell on the other men. "Guys, this is Tyler, an old marine buddy of mine. He's going to drive us to the destination." Then he threw a hand up to the pilot, giving him a command to go.

As the chopper blades whirled to life, all of them climbed into the SUV.

Cole jerked and bounced with the dips and hills of the rough terrain, and his mind settled on the scene they might encounter at his brother's house. He could only pray they'd find Barbara alive and well, but the sinking feeling in the pit of his gut told a different tale. Maybe he should have dropped off the money and hoped for the best.

Don't be an idiot. You damn well know they still would have let her die. Besides, it was a little late for that since the two hours they'd given him to drop the ransom off had already come and gone. It was stupid to concentrate his energy on wasteful thoughts. They were taking the right approach, even if the outcome had yet to be determined. He trusted Dylan Cruz knew what he was doing. The guy hadn't missed a beat yet.

But damn, he never would have suspected his brother would be behind all this. The question of why he was doing this entered his mind again. The agent had been right. Money couldn't have been the motivation for Dunston's actions. Cole had already offered him more than enough. If his brother wanted to get revenge for some reason unknown to Cole, why wouldn't he have simply planned to kill Jenna instead of ransoming her off? As far as money was concerned, Dunston had only received a one million inheritance from Hershel. How much did he agree to pay Ava? She'd already gotten five-hundred thousand.

And how did Ava single-handedly kidnap Jenna? If the two had gone toe to toe, his wager would have been placed on his fiancée to be the victor. His ex-girlfriend was a high maintenance princess wannabe, while his soon-to-be wife was an intelligent, street-smart girl. Jenna would have never let that weak bitch get the better of her. There was always the consideration a gun could have been used for compliance. But they'd talked about that scenario once, and she knew not to ever get into a vehicle with anyone even if they threatened her with bodily harm. He'd made sure she was aware her chances of survival were slim to none if she did.

No. The only way his fiancée would have lost that battle would have been if she were somehow debilitated.

"We'll be there in another half a mile," Tyler said from his position behind the wheel.

"Here's the plan," Cruz announced, peering back at Cole and Gibbs in the backseat. "We're going to park in a clearing up the road. Me and Tyler will take the back of the house, while you two stakeout the front." He tossed them a two-way radio. "This is how we communicate with each other. No one makes a move until we all agree it's safe to do so. If your phones are on, turn them off now. We don't want the perp to know we're coming."

The SUV veered off the road and rolled to a stop a few yards in. As Cole got out of the vehicle, he noticed how secluded this area was. They were surrounded by towering trees and tall weeds. The night sky stretched out like an endless galaxy, dotted with brightly burning stars. It would have been a sight to behold if he'd had the time to stand around and admire it. But tonight, there were lives in danger. Jenna was trapped in a casket somewhere under the ground, probably doing all she could not to fall completely apart. She was clinging to hope someone would find her, and she'd be rescued. This group of four men were assigned that task. And dammit, if it took every bit of resolve he had, he'd see it through.

After hiking through the woods, a small subdivision came into view at the bottom of the hill. Streetlights glowed in the distance, reflecting light off rooftops. Cole could tell the houses in this development were huge. He peered over to find Tyler and Cruz unrolling what appeared to be a blueprint of some kind. Upon closer inspection, he realized it was a sketch of the landscape down below. Gibbs pointed at a dwelling in the center of the drawing. The house number was as clear as a bell. It was the place they were looking for.

"We can come in through here," Cole suggested, running his finger along a trail from the back leading up to the house in question.

They all nodded in agreement, and Tyler rolled up the blueprint and stuffed it inside his camouflage vest.

They cautiously made their way and finally arrived within a few yards of Dunston's house. Cruz held up his hand to him and Gibbs who were bringing up the rear. He glanced back, and without a sound, sliced his hand through the air toward the front of the house in a gesture for them to take up that flank. Cole nodded, and they split up in groups of two, Tyler and Cruz slipping off into the night to the back of the property as they'd discussed in the SUV.

Cole slid his Glock free from the holster and held the butt of it tight against his chest, as Gibbs took up the same position next to him. They slowly side-stepped along the tall hedges lining the front perimeter of the property until coming upon a break in the shrubs. A huge iron gate stood open, and the blacktop of a driveway became visible. When Cole peered around the corner, he saw the vast, dark skeleton of Dunston's house sitting off into the distance. A soft light flickered from one of the windows. It had to be a candle.

Just as Cruz suspected, the electricity had not been turned on yet. The white aluminum panels of what he imagined was a moving van glistened in the moonlight, sitting off to the right side of the house. Although his brother's clunker wasn't anywhere around, Ava's apple-red sports car was parked at the end of the driveway.

He faced Gibbs and whispered, "You take the left side, and I'll take the right."

His partner, in a crouched position, quickly scurried across the yard, hiding behind thick bushes after clearing the opening. He nodded at Cole, giving him the-all clear, and Cole slipped around the corner, heading for more hedge bushes. With his back planted against them, he continued to side-step, closing a decent amount of distance in seconds.

Now he had a clear eyeshot of the moving van. The large rear doors stood open; a beam of light shone from the truck floor. Who would leave a flashlight turned on just lying there? A person who dropped it in a hurry.

Then he noticed a few boxes scattered about, as if they had been tossed up into the air and left to land where they may. Something happened inside the cargo area of that van. Someone dropped everything they had in their hands and didn't bother going back to pick any of it up or couldn't go back and pick any of it up.

Apprehension crawled up Cole's spine like a hairy tarantula. Ava being here meant they'd done something to Barbara. Jenna's best friend would have instantly questioned how Dunston knew this woman, and what she was doing at his house. Did one or both converge on her while she'd been unpacking items in the moving van? If that happened, what kind of fate awaited her after she'd been attacked?

Not a sound or movement stirred from the house, only the steady, quivering light of the candle he now clearly identified through the window.

His radio crackled, and he snatched it from his shirt pocket. *"We're in,"* Cruz said. *"Do you read? We're in the house."*

"What happened to, no one makes a move until we all agree it's safe to do so?" Cole whispered with emphasis.

"Sorry. The back door was open. I saw my chance and I took it."

"Are any of the suspects in the house?" Cole recognized Gibbs' voice.

"We've identified the female suspect. She's on the couch and she doesn't have a pulse," Cruz informed them.

Cole was stunned. "You're telling me Ava Kingsley is dead in there?"

"It looks that way. The downstairs is clear. Tyler is checking the upstairs now."

"I'm coming in," Cole warned, cautiously heading that way.

He and Gibbs met at the front door and Cole tested the knob. It wasn't locked. His partner stood across from him, and they faced each other, nodding. They raised their weapons at the same time, and Cole flung the door open.

They crashed through the opening, spreading out, both instantaneously doing a quick perimeter sweep. Cole lowered his gun the moment he noticed Cruz standing over a body lying across the sofa. Long, blonde hair spilled over the arm of the couch. He ran in that direction.

There wasn't the slightest trickle of blood. No bruises. Not a single scratch on her. If he didn't know better, he'd swear Ava had simply fallen asleep. On the table next to her head, sat a long-stemmed glass filled half-way with wine and a lipstick stain smudged against the rim. Cole picked it up and gazed into its pink depths. A white sediment gathered at the base. He jiggled it, and the powder swirled, settling to the bottom when he held it still.

"He poisoned her," he said, setting it back on the table.

Just then, Tyler's voice boomed from their radios. "*I found a victim in the master bedroom. She's got a weak pulse.*"

"Barbara!" Cole hollered, running toward the darkened stairwell and managing to fumble up the steps.

Tyler stood at the end of the hall, training the beam of his flashlight on the landing in front of them to help the guys make their way through the dark. The closer Cole got he realized the tall ex-marine had a phone to his ear. From the sound of it, he was talking to a 911 operator.

The shuffling of feet echoed behind him, telling Cole that Gibbs and Cruz were close on his heels. Cole was the first one to approach the body. And as Cruz held his light in place, Cole shrank to his knees, grabbed Barb's wrist, and waited for a pulse. It was there, but, Jesus, it was faint.

"Oh, God, Barb. What did he do to you?"

His attention brushed across a severe gash on her forehead, close to her scalp. A lot of blood spilled from the wound, turning her blonde hair crimson, and puddling on the floor beside her face. Her body was warm, so he doubted she'd been here long.

Cole peered up at Cruz. "Put an APB out on this bastard's car. I'm going to find him, and when I do, if he doesn't tell me where Jenna is, I swear to God I'm going to kill him with my bare hands."

As Cole fought to control the rage tearing through him, sirens wailed in the distance. He could only hope and pray to God it wasn't too late for Barbara. She didn't deserve to get caught up in this shit.

Chapter Eleven

"Jenna...Jenna." The soft voice floated on the air, like an angel calling to her from the heavens. "You have to wake up, Jenna."

Her eyes snapped open, and through the darkness, a strong presence lingered with an undeniable force. She'd dozed off in the makeshift casket, and now that something had awakened her, a cold draft infiltrated the tiny space, bringing goosebumps to the surface of her flesh. Panic struck with a mighty blow. What had changed since she'd drifted off to sleep? Why was it so cold in here?

"Jenna, can you hear me?"

Her pulse pounded in her ears. "Who...who's there?"

A faint buzzing echoed throughout the confined area she'd been trapped in for God knows how long, and she was aware of what the sound meant. Any second, the light at the foot of the casket would come on. But it would only last fifteen minutes before the timer would run out, leaving her in total darkness again.

Light radiated from the bulb, as the infrared digits above her face sprang to life simultaneously. "Thank God, you can hear me," the voice said.

She peered over to see Barbara lying beside her. Blood crusted around a large wound in her forehead, and dried, crimson streaks trailed down her face. A spine-tingling scream burst from her like an artillery shell being shot from a cannon on the 4th of July. She covered her face, desperately hoping the gruesome image she just glimpsed would disappear when she removed her hands.

"Why are you screaming? It's just me, for God's sake."

"You're still here?"

"I wouldn't be talking to you if I wasn't still here, dumbass."

"You're not real. I'm still asleep. I must be dreaming."

"Let's hope not. People tend to die when you dream."

"Are you?" Jenna asked, squeezing her eyes shut even though her hands covered her face.

"Am I what?"

"Dead?"

A sigh and then, "I don't know."

Jenna gently removed her hands, braving a stare in Barbara's direction, figuring if this were an illusion, it was a welcome reprieve from the isolation she'd been dealing with ever since Ava knocked her out and stuck her in this grave.

"You look terrible," she told Barb.

"Gee thanks, bestie. But if I'm dead, how am I supposed to look?"

"A little pale maybe. But not horror flick gory like that. You've got a nasty wound on your head, and blood all over your face."

Barbara's attention floated toward the ceiling. "It's just my luck. The first time in ten years I finally find a man I really like, and he kills me, or tries to kill me…I'm really not sure which at this point."

"Are you saying Dunston tried to kill you?"

"That son-of-a-bitch dragged me into his house and bludgeoned me."

"Oh, my God!" Jenna yelped. "I think I saw it happen in my vision."

"A little heads-up would have been nice, ya know."

"I didn't know it was him or you. It was dark in the house, and I didn't see any faces."

"A lot of good your visions do."

"Tell me about it." She swallowed the tears threatening to turn her into a blubbering idiot again. As if she hadn't shed enough of those today. "Professor Delaney calls my visions a gift, but I think they're a curse. Look how they've come between me and Cole."

"I talked to him, you should know. He regretted not listening to you. And I do, too." She took a deep breath, and when she glanced at Jenna again, guilt pinched the corners of her face. "I'm sorry. We should have taken you seriously. You saw this whole thing, and we tried to convince you it wasn't what you thought."

"What happened, Barbara? Why did Dunston do this to you?"

"Ava showed up at his house. I was grabbing boxes out of the moving van when she drove up. I don't think she knew I was there. She was freaking out, going on about how she was in over her head, that she had you in the trunk of her car, and she demanded the rest of her money for kidnapping you."

"Dunston put her up to this. And Cole has no idea his brother is involved." The way things were right now, with Barbara in this condition, and Jenna buried alive in this Godforsaken hole in the ground, if neither one of them made it out of this alive, Cole would likely never learn the truth. Unless he took Ava into custody, and she spilled the beans.

"Like an idiot," Barb continued, "when I overheard what was going on, I was so stunned, I dropped the boxes in my hands. Then Dunston knew I was in there, and I'd heard everything."

After her confession, she closed her eyes and shuddered, as if reliving the terror was unbearable. In a broken voice, she said, "I didn't even make it out of the van before he charged in after me. You should have seen the look in his eyes. I swear, it was the coldest, most hateful glower I'd ever stared into. I just knew he was going to kill me, and he never cared for me at all. I've never felt so utterly betrayed in all of my life."

"I'm so sorry, Barb. I don't know why he turned out to be so evil. It's senseless because Cole was going to split the sale of the business with him. He didn't need to do any of this. I don't understand it. But he had to have planned this from the beginning. Why else would he have solicited Ava's help? I don't even know how he found out she was Cole's ex-girlfriend."

Tears spilled down Jenna's face, and she sniffled. "I'm probably not getting out of here alive."

"Don't say that. You—"

"C'mon. We both know it's hopeless." She swiped at her tears. "I'm going to lie in here until that timeclock," she said, staring at the infrared digits ticking away above her head, "reaches zero. Then I'm going to die. But at least I have you, and I don't have to go alone. I'm grateful for that."

"Oh, Jenna, being your best friend has given me more happiness than you could ever know. I was so glad when you came back to Texas. And I know Cole and I never really got along. But I never questioned how perfect he is for you, and how much he loves you. When you two reunited, things were set right again, just like they should have been a long time ago."

Jenna grabbed Barb's hand, but it was like touching cold air. That's when it hit her, her best friend was probably dead, but for some reason, she hadn't moved on. "Why did you come here?"

She shrugged. "I dunno. For some reason I was drawn here."

Jenna found the strength to laugh with irony. "I don't even know where *here* is."

"The address on the mailbox is eighty-nine Cypress Lane."

"What?" She was blown away. "Are you sure?"

"I'm positive."

She faced Barbara. The insanity of the discovery sank. "Don't you remember? This is the house Cole's father, Joseph lived in. This was where he took Emily hostage, and where Cole rescued her."

"Oh, my God, Jenna. You're right. This is the place, isn't it?"

"Where did they bury me?" she wanted to know.

"You're in the backyard behind the house."

"I'm guessing there's a ventilator hose above ground. Can you see it from the road?"

Barbara shook her head. "No, honey, you can't."

What kind of sick person was Dunston to have used the address of his psychotic father to bury her? Cole would never guess she was here, would he? There would be no reason to come searching for her at this place.

Her heart sank, and tears for the life she might have had with Cole continued to pour out of her. Her time with him had been heaven for as long as she was allowed to have it. The biggest regret was the argument they'd gotten into this morning. He would never know she didn't hold it against him. She hoped for his sake, he wouldn't dwell on it, that he would remember her for the love they shared. If God granted her one final wish before he took her home, she'd go to Cole for the last time, tell him how full he'd made her life, and loving him and having his daughter had been her greatest achievement.

Emily's smiling face entered her mind. For ten years it had been the two of them against the world. Caring for that little girl had given her a reason to get out of bed every morning, when she'd missed Cole so badly all she wanted to do was crawl into a hole and give up. It had been because of the love her daughter brought into her life she hadn't. Emily saved her from herself so many times, giving her a reason to go on when she didn't want to. She would miss them with all her heart. Her only saving grace was she realized Cole was an excellent father. He would be strong for Emily. They would lean on each other like they had done during the time she'd been unconscious in the hospital after her car accident. They would get through this struggle together, as a family. At least she had that.

"Stay with me till the end. Don't leave me, Barbara."

"You are going to survive this, Jenna. I know it in my heart."

"Just promise me, please. I don't want to die alone."

"Okay. I won't leave you. I promise."

"Thank you."

"I love you, Jenna."

"I love you too, Barb."

****

According to the clock on the wall in the hospital corridor, it was a little past five a.m. Cole sat restlessly at the post he'd taken up outside the ICU unit where they'd taken Barbara. The blow to her head put her in a coma, but the scans detected brain activity. He'd been here for hours and was working on his third cup of coffee. While Cruz and Tyler headed to the SUV to get an hour or two of shuteye, he'd been roaming the halls, pacing back and forth, hoping Barb would miraculously snap out of her unconscious state and tell him where Jenna was, if she even knew.

How much information could she have learned before Dunston attacked her? Ava showed up on the scene. Considering the disarray inside the moving van, Barb had to have been in there when his ex-girlfriend drove up. That would have tipped her off something was amiss. From the appearance of the scattered boxes, his brother confronted Jenna's best friend right there, before she'd had a chance to escape. The horror she must have experienced was a disturbing thought. No doubt the woman fought for her life. But it wouldn't have taken much for Dunston, and possibly Ava, to have overpowered her. And Jenna saw the whole thing in a vision. He hadn't taken her seriously.

Stop it. Now is not the time to do this to yourself. There was no time for a pity-party. Jenna's life hung in the balance, and the clock was running out.

"Hey, man," Gibbs said, approaching him. "Why

don't you head to the SUV and try to get a little sleep. Sitting here like this isn't going to make Barbara wake up any faster."

"You think I should rest while Jenna is buried out there somewhere, thinking she's going to die."

Gibbs groaned, dropping his arms to his sides, saying nothing.

Cole peered up at him. "What about you? Why aren't you sleeping?"

"Fuck that."

"Exactly."

"You look like shit."

"That makes two of us."

Gibbs leaned against the wall beside where Cole sat. "We're going to find her."

"Can you put that in writing because it hasn't happened yet. And I'm sick to death we're going to be too late."

Gibbs glanced at his watch. "We still have about thirteen hours."

Cole snorted. "Yeah, if my brother hasn't shortened her time like he threatened to do in the ransom letter. I didn't drop off the money. He has to know that by now."

"I don't think he cares about the money. It's all falling apart on him. That's why he killed Ava and tried to murder Barbara. She found out the truth. And I'll bet Ava panicked. She became a loose cannon, and he couldn't risk her blowing this thing sky high. He's on the run right now. I'd guarantee it."

"Yeah. That makes me feel a whole lot better. The only person left who is either alive or conscious and knows where Jenna is, is making a run for it."

"My point is, he wouldn't have bothered to go back to the burial site. He may not have even checked to see if you dropped off the money."

Cruz's words ran through his mind. *This isn't about the money.*

Obviously, events occurred that his brother hadn't expected. His plan was coming apart at the seams. Just the way they typically did in a ransom situation. His partner was probably right. Dunston bailed when things spun out of control. But he still wasn't any closer to finding Jenna. They'd hit a brick wall. And if something didn't give...

"Hey!" someone hollered.

They both spun toward the disturbance, and Tyler was jogging down the hall. "I've been looking everywhere for you two," he said, out of breath by the time he stood in front of them.

Alarmed, Cole stood up, wondering what happened, but positive there'd been a break in the case, nonetheless. Good or bad, he couldn't be sure.

"A hit came in for Dunston's car. It's been spotted at DFW airport." The guy took a second to catch his breath and leaned against the wall. "He's in custody. They have him at the Arlington PD. Cruz has the SUV fired up and ready to go."

****

Cole stood with Cruz, Tyler, and Gibbs on the opposite side of the partially reflective glass as two Arlington Police detectives interrogated Dunston Rainwater. The smug expression dripping from his brother's face made him want to storm in there and bash the bastard's head in. He knew where Jenna was buried, but from the appearance of things, he wasn't giving up that information.

He faced Gibbs and said between clenched teeth, "When are they going to let me in there with him?"

"Probably never. They know you're his brother. They figure you're too emotionally involved, and you'll make matters worse."

Of course, they did. He would have come to the same conclusion if he had been in their shoes. But he wasn't, and time wouldn't slow down long enough for them to pull their heads out of their asses and realize the approach they were taking wasn't working. "They're not getting anywhere. And they've been in there with him, what, going on two hours now?"

"This is why I was hoping to keep other departments from getting involved," Cruz piped up and said, "But they arrested him on their turf. He committed crimes here as well."

"And he was involved in a kidnapping in another jurisdiction," Cole argued. "The victim has yet to be recovered. So, where does that leave us?"

"You're preaching to the choir," Cruz answered, throwing out his hands.

Cole shook his head in absolute defiance. He'd be damned if they were going to get away with thwarting Jenna's only chance at rescue over some pissing contest with jurisdiction. "Screw this! I'm going in there, and it's going to take the entire Arlington Police Department to stop me." He headed toward the door of the interrogation room.

Two department officers stepped in front of him, blocking his path. "We can't let you go in there, Detective," the burly one warned.

Cole was not deterred. "You need to get the fuck

out of my way if you know what's good for you."

"Wait," Cruz said, interrupting the testosterone battle that was about to blow up like two wolves clashing over leader of the pack status. "There might be something I can do. Just give me five minutes, will you?"

Cole stared down the beefy cop for a solid minute. He could tell the huge bastard wasn't backing down, but neither was he. And he had a whole lot more on the line than this asshole did.

"A few minutes isn't going to make or break you," Cruz reasoned.

"Five minutes," Cole said, "And then I'm either going to tear this place apart, or they're going to let me in there." His heated stare never wavered from the determined eyes of the cop, until the guy finally glanced away.

"That's all I need." Cruz took out his phone and stepped out of the room.

Cole calmed down a little, wandered over to a chair, and sat down, his attention steady on the clock hanging from the wall. Out of the corner of his eye, he caught a glimpse of the two officers who blocked his path earlier step away from their positions and reclaim their places, leaning against the desk on the opposite side of the room. No one said a word.

Four-and-a-half minutes ticked by when someone strolled through the door. A man in uniform approached Cole, and he stood, preparing for the fight of his life if need be. "Detective Rainwater," the man said in a deep voice, "I'm Sergeant Cunningham. We're going to clear the two detectives out of the interrogation room, and you can go in and talk to your brother."

Relief washed over Cole. He didn't know who Cruz talked to, or what strings he'd pulled, but he remained true to his word, and he'd accomplished it with thirty seconds to spare.

Cunningham strode over to the door leading into the room where his brother and the two detectives were, opened the door, and poked his head inside. He spoke a few words, and the reaction of the detectives told Cole they were not happy.

Who gave a shit? He peered over at the brawny cop who gave him a hard time earlier. The guy stared straight ahead, not saying anything, the hint of annoyance on his face. But Gibbs was grinning from ear to ear when he glanced his way. "Screw these assholes," his partner mouthed, as Cole rose from the chair and stepped toward the interrogation room.

The two detectives stepped out of the room, stopped when they saw Cole standing there, glared at him as if they had the power to peel layers from his face, and then filed past him. "I don't know what authority some people think they have," one of them mumbled before leaving the room.

Cole smirked. *Apparently, the kind of authority that got your asses booted out of there.*

The sergeant stepped aside and held the door open for Cole to enter. When he did, his attention fell to his brother, who had the audacity to appear pleased by his presence.

"Well, well," Dunston said, his voice as thick as molasses, "I was wondering when they'd send you in here. I was hoping we could have a little chat, you know, before they lock me up and throw away the key."

"Cut the shit," Cole said, shrinking down into one

of the chairs across from him. "Where did you bury Jenna?"

"Whoa. You work a lot faster than they do," he said, raising his manacled hands toward the huge window, where he probably suspected the other two detectives where watching. "Do you suppose they'll get any pointers from you. Because I have to say, they really suck at their jobs."

"I wouldn't know," Cole answered without batting an eyelash. "They left the room."

"Too bad. Some people don't want to better themselves. Not like you, though, right? You're good at your job. Only I'm better. I took Jenna right under your nose."

A sweltering fire burned a trail through Cole's insides. It was nearly impossible to remain in his chair. He pictured his hands wrapping around Dunston's neck while he strangled the life out of him. But he realized the punk was trying to rattle him. He had to stay focused on the objective. Even if it took nerves of steel to get through this. "You're right. I never suspected you, right up until I found the envelope Ava trashed at the motel with the dog tags you gave her."

Dunston threw back his head and laughter filled the room. When he recovered, he glared at Cole and said, "There's no getting rid of those damn things, is there? Our great-grandpappy tried to pawn them off on me. I swear, they're a curse. They killed him, got me busted, and look what they did to Ava."

"No. That was you."

"Yeah. That was me, wasn't it? But perhaps, if I hadn't given them to her, the bitch wouldn't have gone bonkers like she did."

"That what happened? She go batshit crazy on you? Is that why you killed her?"

Dunston half nodded, as if he had no plans to deny Cole's assumption. He seemed to be enjoying himself far too much. "Everything was rolling along as planned until looney girl showed up at my house while Barbara was there. She was flipping out. You should have seen her," he said, stifling a laugh. "She'd just kidnapped Jenna, and she was paranoid you were going to find her. Boy, you must have really laid it on that bitch at the coffee shop. What'd you do to her anyhow?"

"You know, the same thing these assholes were doing to you in here."

Dunston frowned, appearing impressed. "So, that shit really works on people, huh?"

"You'd be surprised how well."

"I'll be go to Hell."

It amazed Cole how at ease this lunatic was, given his circumstances. He probably wouldn't see the outside of a cell for the remainder of his life. Yet he acted as if this was a normal conversation between brothers.

"We know you paid Ava five hundred thousand to kidnap Jenna. How much more were you going to give her?"

"That was up to you, really. It depended on whether you paid the ransom. Out of curiosity, did you drop off the money? Ava was supposed to go after it. But she ended up a little dead."

"You said she came to your house acting crazy. We found her on your sofa with a glass of poisoned wine by her head."

"After I had to kill Barbara, she was a total basket-case. It took me twenty minutes to calm her down. I finally convinced her to come into the house and fixed her a glass of wine with one too many sleeping pills in it. I'd already had to chase one bitch down and kill her. I didn't have the energy for a second go-around.

"How did you know Ava and I had a past?" It was a question that had been nagging Cole ever since he discovered Dunston was involved in Jenna's kidnapping.

His brother's eyes grew large with irony. "That was a freak accident if you can believe it. I wandered into a local bar the first night I came to town. And wouldn't you know it, she was sitting all alone at a table. She seemed like a good lay, and I was up for it, so I bought her a drink. We got to talking. When I told her my name, she said she'd dated a guy named Cole Rainwater once. The more she told me about you guys, the easier I knew it would be to draw her into my plan. She had one helluva grudge against you. You'll be happy to know I never slept with her though because that would be just...weird."

What Dunston told him fit perfectly with the clues he'd been stumbling across this whole time. Ava running into him and Jenna in the restaurant that day was no chance meeting. She had gotten that job as a wedding planner and slipped a brochure she'd created herself into his mailbox to lure Jenna into her little trap. And it worked. They pulled the wool over his eyes for as long as they'd needed to. The seething anger he'd been holding at bay crept out when he said between gritted teeth, "It was never about the money, was it?"

The amusement Dunston had been displaying disappeared in an instant. His eyes grew dark and brooding, as if there was a demon hiding in the pit of his soul, waiting for its moment to leap out and devour its opponent. "Let me tell you something, you slimy, little maggot, I couldn't have hated you more if you had been my bitch of a mother. She fuckin' worshipped you. *'Dunston, you worthless shit, why can't you be more like your brother?'* " he said, his voice raising an octave as if impersonating someone. " *'He's going to be somebody. And you're just like your crazy father who's locked away in a loony bin. I should have listened to my mother and aborted you. You'll never be half the man he'll grow up to be.'* "

If someone had snuck up behind Cole and hit him over the head with a two-by-four, he wouldn't have been more stunned than he was right now. He never could have guessed his mother was that horrendous. But he had no memory of her. She'd ran off and abandoned him to the vices of his psychopathic father, who had handed him over to Derek Rainwater to raise right before the state locked him away in a mental institution. Was he the only sane one out of the whole family?

Dunston continued with a venomous tone. "I grew up in a house where my mother changed men like she changed underwear. Every one of them were lowlives that beat the shit out of me every chance they could. But you were living it up in your nice house with the white picket fence, decent people to raise you, and a sweet, little girlfriend. How perfect for you!"

How could he have changed things for his brother when he never even knew he existed? No sane person could possibly blame him for Dunston's unfortunate circumstances. "I'm sorry our mother put you through that. If I'd have known you existed, and you were being forced to live like that, I would have moved Heaven and Earth to get you the hell out of there."

His brother shot out of his chair, the chains around his wrists and ankles rattling with the swift movement. He leaned across the table and spit in Cole's face. "Fuck you and your apology! You got to live like a king while I lived in squalor like a dog!"

Cole wiped the spittle from his face as two officers rushed into the room. He held up his hand to stave them off, and Dunston sat back down. "It's okay," he told the cops. "Everything is under control." He stared at them, as if assuring them he could handle this, and they could leave. He still had unfinished business. It was time for his brother to tell him where he buried his fiancée.

After a few minutes of silence, they slowly strode out and left Cole to it. "Where is Jenna, Dunston? It isn't fair to make her pay for this. She's innocent and has done nothing to you."

"She's precious to you, isn't she? Killing her is how I make you pay."

Cole's patience was diminishing by the second. And the clock was ticking for Jenna. He needed to find her before it was too late. "You're going to tell me where she is, or I'm going to make your life so unbearable in prison you're going to wish you were dead."

A big, satisfied grin spread across Dunton's face. "There's nothing you or they," he said, staring pointedly at the massive window, "can do to make me tell you where she is." He faced Cole, unwavering. "You see, Jenna is going to rot in that grave, and you can't save her. Tick tock, big brother."

Red flashed before Cole's eyes when he exploded out of his chair. He was across the table in a heartbeat and had the chains from Dunston's manacles wrapped around his neck, strangling the life out of him.

His brother jerked and writhed, but Cole held his head to the table with a herculean strength he didn't know he had, while he continued to tug on the chains, cutting off his circulation.

The door to the interrogation room slammed against the wall, and several people converged on Cole, tugging on him with excessive force, doing everything they could to pry him loose.

When they finally wrenched him away from Dunston, his purple-faced brother staggered away from the table. Two officers held the man by his arms as he choked and gasped for air. The moment he caught his breath, he flew into a rage. "He tried to kill me! You all saw it!"

Two men grabbed Cole from the back, ushering him toward the door.

Dunston howled with laughter. "Tick tock, motherfucker, tick tock!"

Blind anger swept over Cole again, and he fought the two guys propelling him toward the door to get to his brother one last time.

Two more men sprinted to the rescue, grabbing onto Cole's chest and propelling him backward.

By the time he had been forced out the door and it was securely shut, his head reeled from the potent emotions churning in his gut. His breathing was as heavy as a bull's, and his heart palpitated so hard he was surprised it remained in his chest.

Cruz stepped toward him and clapped a hand on his

shoulder. "It's okay, man. I promised you we'd do all we could to find her, and we will. I'm not giving up hope and neither should you."

Something Cole could not identify crept over him, and he collapsed against Cruz's chest, breaking down and weeping in the silence of the room. He'd held it together so well, doing all he could to be strong for Jenna. But the unthinkable possibility she may die became more real in this moment than at any other time. If that happened, he honestly didn't know if he could go on. She and Emily were his whole world. How in the hell could he tell his daughter he'd let her mother die?

Chapter Twelve

Jenna noticed right away this time when she awoke, the chill she'd experienced when Barbara was here had disappeared. Like before her best friend's visit, the stuffiness inside the box had returned, and sweat coated her skin. Although pitch blackness surrounded her, and she couldn't see her hand if she'd have raised it to her face, she had a sinking premonition Barb was gone. "Barbara?" she said, her voice cracking on a desperate timbre.

Nothingness answered her.

Tears welled in her eyes. She'd promised she wouldn't leave her. But she had, and she found herself alone again.

She squeezed her eyes shut, a guttural wail forcing its way up her throat. "Nooooo! I'm not ready to die!" She pounded her fist against the ceiling of the casket, her mind in a crazed frenzy. "If anybody's out there! Please! I'm down here!" She continued to beat against the raw wood and scream bloody murder until her fists ached, and her voice became hoarse. She couldn't even cry anymore. Her tongue was heavy, throat burned, and her lips were dry and cracked. Hunger pangs wracked her body, and she'd give anything for a sip of water.

The rancid smell of her urine filled her nostrils. But worst of all, the longing in her soul to see Cole one last time tortured her to the point of intolerance. "I'm so sorry," she whispered, as if he were lying right there beside her. "I took our time together for granted. If I could go back, I'd treasure every moment I had with you. I'd live it like it was the last day of our lives." In her grief she called out to God. "If you give me one more chance, I promise I won't squander it. Oh, please. I'll prove to you I'm worthy of it."

The familiar buzzing filled the casket. The light was about to come on. And those dreaded infrared digits would show themselves, letting her know how much longer she would be granted precious life.

Two hours left, and counting down, just like in her cursed vision.

****

The early morning hours had burned off long ago. The rest of the day had ticked by agonizingly slow. Cole reconciled this was how a prisoner on death row must feel, sitting in that tiny cell, eating his last meal, and then waiting for the guards to show up and drag him off to his demise. Only, Jenna was the prisoner waiting to die. Any hope of saving her before the clock ran out had diminished with his brother's resistance.

It didn't matter that they'd combed the more than one hundred acres of Dunston's property in Arlington hoping he'd buried Jenna there somewhere, or that they'd searched several other places his brother might have taken her. They came up empty handed just like he had a suspicion they would. It was obvious Dunston hated him with a fiery passion, even though he couldn't understand it. He would have made damn sure Cole couldn't find her.

Barbara was the last hope to find Jenna. But she hadn't woken from her coma, and even if she did, there hadn't been any guarantee she'd know the location.

Yet, as he rounded the corner to her room, a harsh scream spilled out into the hallway, "Get that needle away from me! Don't you dare come near me with that! I said back the fuck up!"

It sounded just like Barbara. He picked up his pace.

The sight that greeted him when he rushed into her room weakened his knees. Barb sat up in bed, determination chiseled into her face, her arms rod-stiff in front of her as she warded off the nurse coming toward her with a needle.

"What are you doing?" Cole asked, stopping the woman in her tracks.

"Where the hell have you been?" Barbara demanded.

The people in the room, two in blue scrubs and one in a medical coat Coal assumed was the doctor, stared at him as if he was an alien. "We're trying to calm her down," the guy in the white coat with a stethoscope around his neck argued. "She's acting erratically and throwing things at the staff."

So, Barbara was being Barbara.

"They're not listening," she insisted. "I've been telling these assholes for twenty minutes to get you in here."

Cole couldn't resist the grin that popped out on his exhausted face.

"What the hell are you smiling about?" she yelled. "Jenna's buried in a grave somewhere and you're standing around like it's your birthday."

"Do I look like it's my birthday?" Cole retorted, not able to control the irritation this woman evoked in him on a constant basis.

"Then stop lollygagging around and go get her."

"I will!" Cole countered, doing his best not to let this incorrigible woman push him over the edge. "Just as soon as you tell me where she is."

"Fine!"

"Fine!"

"The address is Eighty-Nine Cypress Lane. She's buried in the back yard. You'll see the ventilator hose above the ground."

Cole stood there, stunned. What kind of psychopath would have taken Jenna to the house of his serial killer father to bury her? And why hadn't he considered that scenario?

Barb leveled him with a questioning stare. "You gonna stand there like a brainless moron, or are you gonna go save her?"

Elated, Cole picked up his phone and dialed Cruz's number. Then he eyed the nurse who was still holding the needle. "If I were you, I'd go ahead and give that to her. She'll drive you out of your ever-loving mind if you don't." He situated the phone against his ear and headed toward the door, hearing Barb screaming, "You're an asshole, Cole Rainwater, you know that!"

"We've established that on more occasions than I can count."

****

Time was now nonexistent in this place. The infrared clock had counted down the final two hours, but that seemed like ages ago. She had been surprised she hadn't died within minutes of the clock stopping. Somehow, she was still alive. But it wouldn't be long. The air seemed thicker, harder to consume. Soon she would suffocate to death in the Godforsaken hole in the ground. She had no more tears to shed. The fight had gone out of her. At least she wouldn't suffer anymore. The nightmare, for all it was worth, would finally be over.

But Cole and Emily. How would they take her death? Would anyone ever even find her buried here, in this spot. And if no one ever did, would the people she loved the most ever find closure?

It wasn't about her anymore. Now, it would be about them. They'd have to find the strength to move on without her. Perhaps, God would allow her the opportunity to come and say goodbye one last time. Put their fears and torment to rest. She always envisioned if something were to happen to Cole, he'd find a way to visit her, tell her he was better off where he'd gone, and not to worry about him. But to be happy, knowing they'd be together again someday.

Could she hold a spot for him and Emily in Heaven? Would the Lord let her do that?

Would she go to Heaven? Did she know for certain where people went when they died?

Of course, you know. You always have, haven't you?

What if she'd been wrong all this time? She needed to stop it. A greater divine existed. She'd felt God's presence in her life. Why doubt it now?

Because it was the time for truth. And nobody really knew what they couldn't see. But she would be leaving this Earth, ready or not.

And, God, she wasn't ready. Panic flourished like a wildfire when she realized she could hardly breathe. The beat of her heart slowed, and she closed her eyes, aware death was at her door. Eternal darkness closed in around her, and she couldn't fight the unconsciousness that waited for her.

****

The excavator couldn't haul dirt out of the ground quick enough. Cole paced around the gravesite with his heart in his throat. Heaps of fresh soil piled on top of dried mounds that were already there from when Dunston had originally dug the grave, formed a tall, black wall. The ventilator hose Barbara mentioned, was sticking out of the ground ten inches or more. So, he knew they had the right spot.

The huge machinery digging into the earth whined on, and Cole wanted to jump out of his skin. He couldn't stand this. They needed to dig faster. Every minute that ticked by was a minute without air for Jenna.

"We've got something," Tyler yelled over the loud noise of the excavator. He hopped from the cab, while Cole, Cruz, and Gibbs ran over and peered into the deep hole.

The color of pine was visible under the scattering of black dirt. Cole wasted no time jumping into the gaping hole. "Jenna!" he called, quickly motioning for Cruz to lower the saw.

When he got no response, he swallowed his heart and called out again. "If you can hear me, we're working to get you out! Just hold on for me, honey!"

Cruz handed down the saw and Cole got to work immediately, clearing off a spot, and firing up the tool, being as careful as he could not to cut deep enough to injure Jenna.

When he ripped off the part of the casket he'd sawed into, she lay there, her eyes closed, not moving.

He dove his hand in, placing his fingers against the side of her neck to check for a pulse. There wasn't one. But she was still warm.

"Jesus! I need help to get her out of here. I don't know if she's breathing."

Cruz jumped in beside him, and they both worked to tug her through the large opening. Her body was limp as they held her against the moist earth and hoisted her up as far as they could into the waiting hands of Tyler and Gibbs. The men leaned over the hole, drawing her the rest of the way out.

Gibbs disappeared from Cole's view with Jenna, and Cruz gave him a boost, while Tyler latched onto him, hauling him out.

By the time he stumbled to his feet, Gibbs was leaning over Jenna, giving her chest compressions.

It became strikingly clear at that point she was dead. A stab of intolerable pain shot through him, and he dropped to his knees. The exhaustion in his body threatened to send him collapsing onto the ground, but he clung to the tiniest fiber of willpower that held him upright. His body shook, and his mind swirled with overwhelming emotions. Even though she was gone, he couldn't let her go. His fists pounded the earth, and he wailed in anguish until he was certain his heart would bleed out.

But then, as he witnessed his partner working on her to no avail, something from deep inside his tortured soul urged him to get up, go over there, and do something.

Cole heaved himself off the ground, just when he was convinced he had nothing left, and staggered over to Jenna's crumpled form. He dropped a heavy hand on

Gibbs' shoulder, and his partner peered up. "Let me try," he said in a hoarse voice.

As the guy shuffled away from Jenna, Cole straddled her, and summoning strength from what could only be pure adrenaline, he pressed palms into the center of her chest. "You're not leaving me," he insisted. "I won't let you."

"C'mon, honey! C'mon!" He continued the compressions, refusing to give up. "I know you're in there, and I know you can hear me. Come back to me, Jenna. Don't leave me like this." Tears flowed down his face, as sweat dripped from his forehead.

A few droplets landed on Jenna's check and rolled across her skin as her eyes opened and she gasped for breath.

The sound that burst from Cole was a mixture of excitement and disbelief. He could not describe the relief that washed over him.

Her trembling hand touched his face, and she said in a raspy voice, "Cole? Is it really you?"

He gently cupped both her cheeks, and with a trembling smile, glared down into those baby blue eyes he was afraid he'd never see again. "I'm here, honey, and I swear to God, I'm never leaving your side again."

Tears of joy wracked her weak body. In between sobs, she said, "I thought I was dead."

"You were," Cruz added, gazing down on her. "But he brought you back." He jabbed a thumb in Cole's direction. "It's nice to finally meet you, Jenna. My name is Dylan, and boy, have we been searching all over the place for you."

****

"She's asking for you, Mr. Rainwater."

Cole stood on weak legs, leaving the guys in the waiting room to follow the nurse down the hall to Jenna's room. As they marched on, the woman peered over her shoulder at him and said, "She's doing pretty good considering her ordeal. She was dehydrated, but we're replenishing her fluids now. And she was also starving, so we brought her something up from the cafeteria. I have to warn you, she's a little weak and will need her rest, so you can't stay long, but other than that, she is going to be just fine."

The nurse opened the door to show Cole in, and then left them alone.

Jenna bit into a sandwich and glanced over to see him enter.

A lopsided grin spread across his face. "We have to stop meeting this way," he said, referring to the last time he'd waited in the hospital on pins and needles after her car accident.

She placed her sandwich on the tray. "So, let's make a pact we're not going to do this anymore."

He stepped closer, sitting in the chair next to her bed. "I'm holding up my end of the bargain on that front pretty good, but you on the other hand…"

Her smiling eyes became serious. "Thank you for rescuing me again and saving my life."

He placed his hand over hers, and she squeezed it. "Anytime."

"How did you find me anyhow?"

"Barbara. When she woke up from her coma, she told me where you were."

She gasped, slapping a hand to her mouth. "Oh my God." Her words were muffled under her hand. She removed it and asked, "She's alive?"

234

Cole was confused. "How did you know what happened to her?"

"She came to see me."

"What?"

"Yeah. She had a terrible gash on her forehead, and she said Dunston went after her and hurt her really bad. We honestly weren't sure if she was dead or alive."

"Oh, she's alive," he confirmed. "And ornerier than ever."

"She told me where I was buried." Then she faced Cole, her eyes large with fear. "Where's Dunston?"

"In jail. And he's never getting out. He poisoned Ava. We found her dead at his house."

"She kidnapped me and admitted she was doing it to get money out of you. I didn't know Dunston was involved until Barbara came to visit me, and she told me he was part of it."

"He was the one who hired the PI to take those pictures of me and Ava."

Jenna stared at Cole, puzzlement on her face. "He's your brother. Why did he do such a thing?"

"It wasn't for the money. He ransomed you off to pay Ava for her part in this. He did it because he hated me. Evidently, our mother used to throw me up in his face all the time. To hear him tell it, I was living a great life, while he was going through Hell."

She shook her head, the expression she gave told him she wasn't buying it. "That's insane."

"Hatred can make people do unthinkable things."

"I guess you have a point."

"The one thing I couldn't figure out," Cole said, rubbing his chin, "was how Ava managed to kidnap you."

"I can't put my finger on exactly what happened. But after I listened to your voicemail, I got spooked. So, I gathered my purse and hurried out of Barb's house. I headed toward my car when something overcame me. I swear, it was like I was having a vision at the same time the event was taking place. Something similar occurred when Joseph came after me at the rental, remember? I saw him breaking into the house in a psychic episode at the same time he was doing it. Except this time, I couldn't break out of the vision. I was paralyzed, making it easy for Ava to kidnap me."

Cole lowered his head. "God, I'm sorry, honey, that had to be horrifying."

"Not as horrifying as lying in that casket knowing I was going to die." Her voice caught on a whimper. "I was so worried about you and Emily," she admitted, tears streaming down her face. "How you two were going to move on without me. I prayed God would give me one more chance. I would have given anything to see you again."

"Hush now," he said, moving in and kissing her cheek. "I'm here, and you're seeing me now. Trust me, that isn't ever going to change."

Once he settled back into the chair, it hit him how close he'd come to losing her again. All the torment he'd experienced over the last twenty-six hours, reconciling with the fact she would probably die, and he was powerless to stop it. He'd never been so helpless and vulnerable in his entire life. He cleared his throat, doing his best to hold the tears at bay, even though one slipped out and ran down his cheek. "I wanted to apologize."

She stared at him, drew him closer, and wiped the

tear from his eye. "You have nothing to apologize for. I shouldn't have been so hard on you. When I started having these visions again, I didn't want to believe it either. We were so happy, and then…"

He shook his head, refusing to give himself a pass on his actions. "I should have believed in you. In my heart I knew better. But I didn't want to accept this could happen to us all over again."

"It sounds like neither one of us wanted to accept it. I'm sorry I put you in the position I did by insisting we hire your ex-girlfriend as our wedding planner." She peered off into the distance. "I guess I wanted to show you I could handle it. You know, that I wasn't jealous. But deep down, the thought of you being with another woman made me envious, even though I tried to convince myself it didn't. I just wanted us to have the kind of relationship we could be secure in."

"Hey," he said, gently taking her chin and turning her to face him. "Do you think the thought of you being with another man doesn't make me crazy? Before I knew Emily was mine, I was beside myself with jealousy thinking you had a child with another guy. Just because we're envious of the opposite sex showing the other one attention, doesn't mean we don't have a healthy relationship. Your having been jealous of Ava shows you love me. If that didn't bother you, how much could you have cared about me?"

A smile found its way through the worried storm clouds in her eyes. "When I was fifteen, I thought I couldn't have loved you more. But I was wrong. I love you more than that each passing day. My love for you has only grown over time. It can never lessen."

He lifted her hand to his lips and kissed it, saying,

"Let me tell you something, lady, you and our daughter live right here." Then he placed her hand over his heart. "I would lay down my life for either one of you and not give it a second thought. There isn't anyone else I would do that for. If that isn't true, unconditional love, I don't know what is. I love you, Jenna. That won't change twenty years from now, and it still won't change when I'm ninety." He brushed an auburn strand of hair from her face, and she caught his hand, cradling it against her cheek.

Just then, loud voices erupted from the hallway, right outside Jenna's room.

"Ma'am, you're not supposed to be out of your room. What are you doing?"

"My best friend is in that room, and if you think you're going to stop me from seeing her, you've got another thing coming."

Jenna and Cole stared at each other and said in unison, "Barbara."

She barged through the door, a nurse on her heels. "I'm sorry," the woman said, in reference to the patient who had rudely interrupted them.

"So, what," Barb said, turning her annoyed expression on Cole, "do you think you can have her all to yourself."

Cole glanced at the flabbergasted nurse. "I'm guessing you didn't give her that shot after all."

"Hell no, they didn't," Barbara answered for her.

"Welp, don't say I didn't warn you," Cole said, rising to his feet and kissing Jenna on the cheek. "I'll see you later, honey. Get some rest."

As he brushed past the two standing by the door, the nurse grabbed Barbara's arm. "Okay, miss, you're coming with me."

He'd made it to the other side of the door when Barbara's voice spilled out again. "If you don't get your hands off me, lady, you're going to draw back a nub."

He smiled to himself, figuring the world was set right again, and strode on.

****

Jenna peered through the small, thick window of the door leading into the visitor's room at the county jail. Dunston sat there in an orange jumpsuit, chained to a long table, his head lowered, and foot tapping.

She nodded at the guard to let her in. A buzzer sounded and the door opened.

When he peered over at her, the shock that lit his face was the best gift in the world. "Hello, Dunston," she said, sitting down at the far end of the table. "You surprised to see me?"

"What…who…how…"

"It wasn't easy crawling out of that grave you put me in. But we have Barbara to thank for that. You see, after you thought you killed her, she came to visit me while she was in a coma. She told me what you did to her. And when she woke up, she told Cole where to find me."

He clamped his mouth shut, sat there a minute, then said, "What are you doing here? I didn't put any visitors on my list. You're not supposed to be here."

The door buzzed again, and in marched Cole. He strolled around behind Jenna and placed his hands on her shoulders. "Those are the perks of being in law enforcement. They let me call in a favor every now and then. This is one of those times."

Dunston lowered his head again. Jenna could tell

he was seething. "What do you want?"

Cole answered. "We just wanted to drop by and let you know we've decided we no longer want you to be best man for our wedding."

He didn't respond. Only sat there, his face becoming red.

"In fact," Cole continued, "we've already replaced you—"

The buzzer sounded out again, and Cruz waltzed in. "With me," the Texas Ranger finished for Cole. "I'll be the one making sure your stay here is memorable."

Dunston finally peered up and snorted. "You won't get away with pulling any shit. They already assigned me an attorney, asshole."

The buzzer sounded out for the third time. Angelo Berlusconi trudged into the room. "That would be me, sonny."

"Little brother, meet your attorney, Angelo Berlusconi," Cole announced. "He's got a helluva background in criminal defense. Nowadays he specializes in business though. Got me every penny for the sale of my company shares. You know, the business ol' Great-grandpappy left me that I sold and was going to split the proceeds with you."

The haughty expression on Dunston's face fled like a robber from the scene. He leveled Cole with a hateful glower. "That's bullshit. You can't railroad me like that. I've got money. I'll just hire another attorney."

Cole said, "Your money's out there and you're in here. Who are you going to call to take care of that for you? I bet Ava would have helped you out. But you killed her."

Dunston shot out of his chair. His body shook with

fury as he pounded on the table with every furious word that poured over his lips. "You! Can't! Do! That!" Spittle flew from his mouth.

Three guards entered the room from a side door, quickly approaching the out-of-control inmate. His brother took notice of them and sat back down, pulling himself together.

Jenna got up and strolled to the door with Cruz, the attorney, and Cole following behind.

As they reached it, Cole spun around, glared at Dunston, and said, "You know, the whole time you had my fiancée buried six feet under the ground, I was afraid time would run out before I could find her. But in here," he remarked, throwing out his hands to their surroundings, "you have all the time in the world. Tick tock, motherfucker, tick tock."

A word about the author...

Although not a native Texan, Donnette Smith has spent more than half her life living in the Lone Star State. She is an entrepreneur and former business owner of Tailor Maid Services LLC. After spending a few years working as a journalist for the *Blue Ridge Tribune*, she realized her love for writing romantic detective novels. Her stories cover a wide range of genres, from horror, time travel, mystery, fantasy, paranormal, and thriller. But one theme stays the same, there is always a detective solving a crime, and a gorgeous victim he would lay down his life to protect. Donnette's biggest fascination is with forensic science and crime scene investigations. Her first mystery/suspense novel, Lady Gabriella, was published in 2008. Her second novel was a horror/mystery/suspense titled Cunja and debuted in 2012. Her third novel, Killing Dreams, book one of The Spirit Walkers series, is a fantasy story released in 2021. Her newest novel, book two of The Spirt Walkers Series is titled, Buried Alive. Donnette plans to add many more upcoming books to The Spirit Walkers Series collection.

www.donnettesmith.com

Thank you for purchasing
this publication of The Wild Rose Press, Inc.

For questions or more information
contact us at
info@thewildrosepress.com.

The Wild Rose Press, Inc.
www.thewildrosepress.com

Printed in the USA
CPSIA information can be obtained
at www.ICGtesting.com
JSHW012104140923
48176JS00005B/88